Texas on My Mind

Texas on My Mind

A Heart of Texas Romance

Eve Gaddy

TULE
PUBLISHING

Chapter One

"DO YOU THINK this dress is too much?" Charlie Stockton asked her sister.

"I think you look amazing in it," Audrey said. "Turner's going to flip when he sees you."

Charlie laughed. "You're kidding, right? Are we talking about the same Turner McBride, one of my oldest friends? I'm not sure he even realizes I'm female."

"Oh, really? Then why did he ask you to the Cancer Society fund-raiser tonight?"

Charlie pushed her hair back from her face. "Because he needed a date. He doesn't have a girlfriend at the moment and we've been friends for a million years." She and Turner had been friends since middle school. Good friends. Even best friends, but never romantically involved. But lately, she'd sensed a change in Turner, in the way he treated her. He was always nice to her, but recently he'd been even nicer than usual. And she'd caught him watching her a few times with a curious expression on his face. But when she asked him about it, he'd told her she was imagining things. So she filed it away to think about later. Because tonight she knew she'd have fun. She always did with Turner.

"Why would it be too much?"

"Because it's so *not* me. But I couldn't help it, I fell in love with it the minute I saw it." She turned from side to side, twisted her head to look at the back and then faced forward to look at herself in the full-length mirror on the door of her bedroom closet. *What a gorgeous dress.* The diaphanous red fabric was shirred across the strapless bodice and waist. The sparkle and glitter of rhinestones traced the neckline of the bodice. Gathered at her hips, the dress flared out in pleats that pooled on the floor.

"Who wouldn't?" Audrey asked. "I've noticed Turner's been hanging around the shop more often."

"Turner likes pie." The Stockton sisters owned and ran Char-Pie, the pie shop on Main Street in Last Stand, Texas.

"You and he have been more chummy than usual. Is there something you want to tell me?"

"What would I have to tell you that you don't already know?"

Audrey raised her eyebrows. "Lots, I'm sure."

"You're imagining things."

Audrey had been lounging on Charlie's bed while watching her get ready, but now she sat up straight and pinned her sister with a narrow-eyed gaze. "Are you sure you and Turner have never been more than friends?"

"What?" She turned her back on the mirror to see if Audrey was kidding. "No, of course not. Oh, I take that back. He kissed me when we were fourteen but I had gum in my mouth and he had braces so it was a disaster. We both about died laughing."

"Yes, but you're not fourteen now and you're both single," Audrey persisted. "And you have to admit, Turner McBride is hot."

Sure, she could admit that. Turner was tall, with blue eyes and medium-length brown hair. With his classic features and a killer smile, he was damn good-looking. Not to mention, he was a successful doctor, a neurosurgeon. She knew he helped out on the McBride family ranch from time to time, which no doubt explained his healthy tan and lean, muscled body. On top of all that, he had the McBride charm, in spades. "I'd have to be blind not to admit Turner is very appealing. He's a sweetheart. But I don't want to lose our friendship and if we actually got together, I'm pretty sure we would."

"Then why are you wearing a dress meant to blow his mind?"

"Because it's gorgeous and I wanted it."

"That's the only reason? No ulterior motive?"

"I wanted the dress so I got it. I wanted to look different. I was tired of always looking blah."

"You sure as hell don't look blah now," Audrey said.

"It's a change, all right. But I'm not out to seduce Turner. You know how I feel about getting involved with a man again." When her ex-husband had walked out on her because she "couldn't give him what he needed," it had cured her of wanting to marry again. In fact, it had almost put her off men entirely. She'd relented on that, at least enough to date casually, but she was doing just fine on her own, thank you.

"If you say so. I'd still pay money to see Turner's face when he gets a load of you wearing this dress."

Charlie studied herself in the mirror again. She looked like a completely different woman from the one who wore jeans and a chef's apron most of the time. Even when she wasn't working at Char-Pie, she generally wore jeans or shorts and a T-shirt or sweater, depending on the weather. Occasionally she wore a dress, though nothing like this number.

"I haven't worn a formal since I lived in California." Which brought to mind her ex again. Why he'd left her and why she wouldn't risk her heart again.

"You're thinking about that bastard Lance again, aren't you?"

"No," she lied.

Audrey raised her eyebrows.

"Not really. It's just that he's so tied to California in my head." Her sister knew exactly how devastated she'd been when her marriage failed. Everyone else, even Turner, only knew she was divorced. She never talked about the reason why. Not to anyone but her sister, anyway. "But it's been over for two years and most of the time I don't give him a single thought."

"I hope not. Lance Archer is not worth a second of your time."

Charlie planned to enjoy being with Turner and ignore the little voice that every now and then wondered if they could ever be more than friends. But they couldn't. Not unless she was willing to risk ruining a lifelong friendship.

"WHO ARE YOU and what have you done with Charlie?" Turner said when Charlie opened the door. This woman was definitely a Charlotte, not Charlie, his good buddy. Not Charlie—one of his best friends, the one he could always count on to either kick his butt or sympathize as needed.

"Very funny." She scowled at him and let him into her house. "I'm still me, even if I'm wearing a formal dress and more makeup than I usually wear in a week."

Turner thought his eyes were going to pop out of his head. He'd been thinking a lot about Charlie lately. But now... Wow. Just...wow. "You look amazing." Her strapless red gown showed off a generous expanse of smooth, creamy skin, from her neck, to her shoulders, to the low-cut bodice with sparkles across the top of it. Like he needed more invitation to look at her breasts? The dress hugged curves he hadn't known she had, flaring out in ruffles at her hips. They weren't frilly ruffles. Instead they sort of swirled around and fanned out gradually from her hips to the floor.

Her face didn't look like hers either. Sure, she was clearly recognizable as Charlie, but not Charlie, his old friend, who he saw often at her pie shop, wearing an apron, with her hair pulled back and flour on her face. Or at the Last Stand Saloon, wearing jeans, boots, and drinking a beer.

No, this woman was pure gorgeous temptation.

"You're staring at me like you've never seen me before. Is it too much?" She waved a hand at her dress.

"Too much? Are you kidding? You look fantastic."

"Let's not get carried away," she said with a laugh. "I'll get my purse and we can go."

Charlie locked her door and turned around, stopping short before she took two steps. "Really? You brought your 'vette?"

Oops. He hadn't thought about Charlie having a hard time getting in and out of the Corvette in a long formal gown. "Sorry. Do you want me to go get my SUV? It won't take long." He drove his small SUV most of the time, especially if he went out to the family ranch. If he tried to drive the 'vette on those roads, it would bottom out in a heartbeat.

"No, I'll just fold up like a pretzel and be fine."

Okay, that was the Charlie he was used to. He shook his head, a little unsettled by his reaction to her. Yes, he'd been thinking about her—about the two of them—a lot lately. But damn, he hadn't expected to be totally blown away when he saw her. "Are you sure? I don't mind."

"Let's just go." She'd walked to the car and was standing beside it. "You're going to have to help me in and out."

"Let me pull the seat back all the way. That should help." Maybe. The dress was fitted on the top but there was a lot of fabric making up the bottom. With his help, she backed up to the car, lowered herself into the seat and swung her legs inside, arranging all the layers of her dress around her. The maneuvering brought their faces close together. He not only got a whiff of her perfume—a sexy, sultry scent that had his stomach clenching—but her eyes were a brilliant green and her lips were plump, red and inviting as hell. He wanted to kiss her. The last, and only, time he'd kissed Charlie they'd been teenagers and it hadn't gone well. They'd laughed themselves sick and gone right back to being friends. But they weren't teenagers anymore and he suspected kissing her now would be a whole lot different.

"Is my dress inside? I don't want you to close the door on it."

"All good. Can you get the seat belt?"

"Yes. Maybe."

He shut her door and went around to the driver's side and got in. Charlie was still struggling with the seat belt so he helped her find the other end and buckle it.

She narrowed her eyes and gave him a death stare. "If you laugh, I'm going to punch you in the nose."

She would do it, too. "Not laughing. I promise."

"I'm glad you asked me to this fund-raiser," Charlie said as he started the car. "I've been to Jameson House before but only to some of the charitable organization offices, not to an event."

Turner's hand tangled in her dress as he shifted. "Charlie?"

"Oh, sorry." She gathered it closer to her. "Is that better?"

He could hardly see her over the mountains of red fabric. "Sort of." He heard her giggle and shot her a dirty look. "So Wallace never took you to anything there?" Rick Wallace, the doctor she'd broken up with a few months ago, was well known for wining and dining his girlfriends. He was also known for being a player, which was why Turner had been glad when he heard they'd broken up. Charlie needed a nice guy to settle down with, not Last Stand's ultimate player.

"No, he didn't. I wanted to but it just never happened. Do you know anything about the history of Jameson House?"

"Not any more than almost anyone in Last Stand knows. The Jamesons were one of the original families who fought in the battle of Last Stand. Ruby Jameson was Jameson III's spinster granddaughter and the only surviving member of her family. She willed the family mansion to the hospital, along with a boatload of money we used to expand it. Which is why we have such an excellent hospital." And why he could practice a specialty like neurosurgery in a small town.

"I didn't know all that. I mean, obviously, the Jamesons were hospital benefactors since the hospital is named after them, but I didn't know the details about Ruby and the family mansion."

"Ask Clara Perkins," Turner said, speaking of the older lady nicknamed *The Matchmaker*. "Clara knows the entire history of the Jamesons. And most everyone else in town too."

Fifteen minutes later, they pulled up to Jameson House. The gracious old Victorian mansion on the edge of town with its wide porch, intricate trim, and winsome turrets was a symbol of another age. Yet it was put to a modern use. A number of charitable organizations had offices there. Fundraisers, like this one for cancer research, and other events, particularly formals, were often held there, too.

There was valet parking. The attendant opened Charlie's

door, then stood there with a bewildered expression on his face. Turner wished he had a picture of it. "Better let me help her out," he told the poor guy.

By the time he got around there, Charlie had managed to swing her legs out, along with a lot of the dress. He held out his hands but Charlie waved them aside. "I can do it myself, but make sure my dress doesn't drag on the street."

"Too bad there's not a red carpet."

"Oh, you're funny. Not."

They walked into the ballroom to a sea of flowers. At least, that's what it looked like to him. Floral centerpieces on the tables, hanging baskets and pots of various colored flowers were placed everywhere. There was even a fountain of, believe it or not, flowers. Each level of the tile and stone fountain held flowers, and flowering vines fell from one level to the next, pooling at the bottom in a riot of color.

"Oh, my God, this is beautiful," Charlie said, sounding a little awestruck.

He turned to look at her with a smart-ass comment on the tip of his tongue but instead he said, "So are you."

He hadn't meant for that to slip out but she really looked gorgeous tonight.

For a moment, Charlie seemed as surprised as he'd been. Then she lifted an eyebrow. "Careful there. I might think this is a real date if you start saying things like that."

"Hate to break it to you, Charlie, but this is a real date."

"A date between friends isn't a real date," she insisted.

Maybe not. But it could be. Turner had been thinking about Charlie a lot recently. Thinking about Charlie and him. And tonight—damn, he was seeing her in a whole new light. Beautiful, desirable. A knockout. *It's that damn red dress and lipstick. And the perfume that smells like sin personified.*

"You're staring at me again. What are you thinking?"

I've been wondering for weeks now if we could be more than friends.

Until she'd broken up with Rick, he hadn't really considered it. He and his last girlfriend had called it quits several months ago and while he'd had some dates, he hadn't found anyone who truly interested him. Then Charlie had broken up with Rick, and ever since then, she'd been on his mind damn near every day. At first he'd ignored the errant thoughts. Sure, he loved Charlie. She was fun and sweet and he'd known her forever. He remembered the times they'd been together and just hung out. Eating burgers and greasy fries and talking about everything under the sun.

He and Charlie knew each other really well. They genuinely liked each other. They tolerated each other's idiosyncrasies. They were both single. He'd never been married and Charlie was divorced. She'd never told him much about her marriage—only that her ex was a bastard and she was glad to be rid of him.

"I'm just thinking about how much I missed you when you lived in California. I'm really glad you came back."

She looked surprised, then a bit mystified. "What brought this on? I've been back for two years."

"I know." He reached out and cupped her cheek. "But I don't think I've ever told you how happy I am that you're living in Last Stand again."

Chapter Two

HER BREATH CAUGHT. Afraid she'd stutter, she didn't even try to speak. Turner had touched her before, of course. Many times. He'd danced with her, patted her shoulder, given her a hug. But he'd never touched her quite like this and looked into her eyes until everything—the room, the noise, the people—faded away and they were alone, with the promise of what might happen between them.

Damn, girl, you are totally imagining this.

Am I?

He wasn't teasing or making light of the situation like he usually did. He was being sincere and she had no clue what to do with that.

She went for sincerity. "I missed you, too." And humor. "Who else is going to make me watch bloody action flicks?"

He smiled. "Would I do that?"

She nodded. "You have before."

"I won't do it again. From now on, only movies you like." He dropped his hand and put it on the small of her back, very lightly. "Come on. Let's find our table."

He was freaking her out a little bit. Maybe even a lot.

Calling her beautiful. Saying he'd missed her. Looking at her as if she wasn't his old friend. Looking at her as if…she could be his lover.

She'd always been careful to not think about Turner in that way. And she could have sworn he'd never thought about her as more than a friend. But maybe she was wrong. Or maybe he never had. Until now.

"Why do I feel like everyone is staring at me?"

He shot her an amused smile. "Because you look fantastic. I thought we'd already established that."

"Thanks, but you're my friend. You have to be nice."

"Being friends doesn't mean I can't recognize a gorgeous woman when I see one."

She stopped and stared at him. He made it sound as if he were saying the most natural thing in the world, rather than flattering her in a way he never had before. She only wished this whole conversation wasn't making her tummy flutter like a demented butterfly was flying around in it.

Thank God, Shane Highwater and Lily Jones walked up to them just then so she didn't have to think of a reply. Lily was a reporter for *The Defender*, Last Stand's local paper. Shane was the chief of police. She was a little surprised to see the two together, since last she'd heard Lily had been out for Shane's blood. But although they weren't hanging on each other or anything, they seemed very much a couple. Then she saw them exchange a scorching look and needed to fan herself. Yep, they were together all right. They all greeted each other and Shane and Turner complained about fundraisers in general and this one specifically, before going off to get some drinks.

"Men," Charlie said. "This is my first time at Jameson House. It's beautiful, isn't it?"

Lily looked around, nodding her agreement. "It's a first for me, too. I love your dress. It's really different."

"Thanks. You should have seen me trying to fit into Turner's Corvette."

Lily laughed out loud. "Oh, I wish I had seen it!"

"Your dress is beautiful," Charlie said. Lily was stunning. Her long auburn hair was fashioned into an intricate French braid and the teal chiffon V-neck dress with its lacy see-through back looked like it had been made just for her.

"Thank you."

"Are you doing an article for the newspaper?"

"Yes, but not like my usual ones. This one will be a human interest story." She dimpled. "I uh, convinced Shane to come with me."

"He didn't look like he considered it an imposition," she said dryly. "He complained but that seemed perfunctory."

Lily laughed. "Honestly, I didn't have to twist his arm too much."

"I could see that," Charlie said, and they both laughed.

They chatted a little and then Lily said, looking over Charlie's shoulder, "Here comes Rick Wallace. I guess you two aren't dating anymore? Since you're here with Turner, I mean."

"We're not, but we're still friendly." Rick was an ER doctor who Charlie had dated for a while and broken up with several weeks before.

"Well, this is my lucky day," Rick said as he reached them. "Two beautiful unattended ladies."

"Sorry to crush your dream but we're not unattended," Charlie said. "Our dates went to get us drinks."

"Oh, there's Rebecca St. James," Lily said. "I don't mean to be rude, but I'd really like to talk to her." She started to leave, then said a little shyly, "When Shane comes back, can you tell him where I am? Nice to see you, Rick."

"Sure thing."

"I'm glad she left," Rick said watching her go before he turned back to Charlie.

"Why? I like Lily."

"I have no problem with her but I wanted to be alone with you."

"Why?" Charlie asked suspiciously.

"You look sensational."

"Thanks," she said a little warily.

"What do you say we skip this boring dinner and go somewhere more fun?"

Charlie laughed and shook her head. "You really are incorrigible."

"It's one of my best qualities," Rick said. "So what do you say?"

"Thanks but no thanks. I happen to be here with Turner. And you and I, my friend, are no longer dating."

"Turner? I thought you two were buddies from way back. He won't mind if you leave."

"But I will. Go find some other gullible girl to hit on."

"Now, now. No need to be rude."

"Not rude. Truthful. And I'm perfectly happy to be here with Turner."

"What a waste. See you later, gorgeous," Rick said, just as Turner walked up with her drink.

"Hi, Turner."

"Rick. Trying to steal my date?"

Rick laughed. "As a matter of fact, yes, but she wouldn't go for it. I'll take my heartbroken self off." With that he left.

"Oh, please," Charlie said, taking the glass of wine Turner handed her. "He has no heart to break."

"What a douche," Turner said, watching Rick before looking at her.

"I thought you and he were friends?" she said, surprised at his comment.

"We are. Usually. But not when he's being a douche."

"Because he was flirting with me? He didn't mean anything by it."

"Are you really that naive?"

"Naive is the last thing I am. I know Rick and all that flirting means nothing."

Turner shrugged in answer. "If you say so. Let's go. They'll be serving dinner before long."

On their way to their table Charlie saw Emma Corbyn and Red Aldean and waved. They seemed an unlikely pair but they both looked like they were enjoying themselves. Emma looked at home in this setting, though Charlie had to grin when she saw the librarian hide her e-reader. Red, who owned Last Stand Expeditions, looked completely different from his usual outdoorsman persona. In fact, he sure cleaned up nice.

Both she and Turner knew two of the three couples at their table—the Weatherlys, who were around her age, and Mr. and Mrs. Perkins, who were a good bit older. The young couple neither of them knew introduced themselves as Mike and Sherri Thornton. The way they looked at each other, not to mention kissed frequently, made it clear they were still newlyweds.

Charlie had always heard that Turner was a great date. Tonight she discovered why. He was always nice to her, especially if he'd convinced her to go somewhere with him, but somehow, this time felt different. *He* was different.

Clara Perkins, the town matchmaker, and her husband seemed to enjoy themselves and chatted happily to the younger couples. "I'm glad to see your brother Graham and Bella Benson are getting along," Clara said to Turner. "You know I introduced them," she said proudly.

As they talked the servers brought their food—a chicken dish that looked surprisingly good, fluffy mashed potatoes, mixed vegetables and buttered rolls that she could swear were homemade.

"Yes, Graham told me, Mrs. Perkins," Turner said. "You did good there."

"I told your brother and I'll tell you, call me Clara. When you call me Mrs. Perkins it makes me feel like I'm Minna's age," she said speaking of the town's oldest resident.

"Yes, ma'am. Clara."

"You don't appear to need my help finding a date," Clara observed shrewdly.

"No, ma'am. The girl for me is right here." He picked up Charlie's hand and kissed it.

She nearly blushed and started to deny it, but Turner grinned and winked at her so she didn't. Having been on the receiving end of Clara's machinations, she understood why he'd claimed her as his girlfriend. A claim that meant nothing—so why did it make her wonder what it would be like to be Turner's woman for real?

"Where do you work, Charlie?" Sherri asked her.

"My sister and I own a pie shop on Main Street."

"It's wonderful," Charlie's friend Rachel Weatherly said.

"Thanks, Rachel." Rachel was one of her regular customers so Charlie knew she wasn't just blowing smoke.

"I've seen it but haven't been there yet," Sherri said.

"You should go," Turner said. "The Bluebonnet Cafe has nothing on Char-Pie."

Charlie laughed since the Bluebonnet Cafe in Marble Falls was known all over the state, and probably farther for its pies. "Thanks, but I'm sure there are people who'd argue that."

"No, dear," Clara said. "Turner and Rachel are right. Your pies are delicious."

"Thank you," she said again. "Y'all are very sweet."

Once they'd eaten and were listening to the speakers, she turned her head to find Turner looking at her.

"Stop staring at me," she hissed. "You're giving me a complex."

He smothered a laugh. "Sorry," he whispered. But he didn't stop looking.

Getting into Turner's 'vette was easier going home, since she didn't have to worry about messing up her dress. But it was still a tight fit. "Thanks for bringing me tonight. I've wanted to go to Jameson House for a long time."

"Glad you enjoyed it. I did too."

"Then why were you and Shane complaining?"

"That? I have to keep up my rep, you know."

"What rep is that?"

"Jaded doctor."

Charlie laughed. "Hate to break it to you, Turner, but you are so *not* jaded." He frowned at her so she added, "That's a good thing."

At her place, he helped her out of the car and walked to her back door with her. She almost always used the kitchen door. "Did you want to come in for a nightcap?"

"I'll come in for a little bit but I don't need a drink."

"Okay." She opened the door and let them inside. Tossing her purse on the counter, she said, "All right, Turner, what's going on? You've been acting strangely all night."

"How so?"

"I know why you said I was your girlfriend. Every single person in town has been the object of Clara's matchmaking. But you've been treating me like we're on a date. A real date." There. She'd said it. Now to hear what he had to say.

"It was a real date."

"News to me. It wasn't when you asked me."

"Sure it was. I distinctly remember asking if you'd be my date for the fund-raiser."

Since she had no idea how he'd phrased the request she

didn't respond.

"We've been friends a long time," he said.

"Practically forever."

"I've been thinking a lot about you lately," he said. She waited for him to go on. "Have you ever thought about the two of us being more than friends?"

"As in friends with benefits?" Damn it, why did the thought of "benefits" with Turner make her tingle?

"Not exactly. More than that."

"I don't understand."

"We could start seeing each other."

"You mean—you want us to date? Like, go out on dates and everything?" Was he joking? He didn't look like he was kidding.

"Yes. Exactly like that." Hands in his pockets, he lounged against her countertop. He'd taken off his coat and tie and left them in his car. He looked totally relaxed. Totally at home.

Totally hot, damn it.

"What brought this on? You've never been interested in me that way."

"I have, but it's never been the right time. One or both of us have always been involved with someone else."

Setting that aside, since she wasn't sure she believed him, she said, "And you think the right time is now."

"It's worth considering, don't you think?"

"Honestly, Turner, I don't know *what* to think."

He pushed himself away from the counter and walked over to her. His sky-blue eyes were full of devilment as he took her in his arms. "Let's try this."

Her eyes widened. He bent his head down and kissed her.

She was surprised, though she shouldn't have been. Damn, Turner knew how to kiss. Why had she never kissed him other than that one time when they were young teenagers? She couldn't help relaxing—partly because her knees were wobbly—and returning the kiss. His lips were firm, but soft; his tongue made lazy forays into her mouth, exploring it leisurely. He was sampling her like...like she was a delicious piece of pie. She tangled her tongue with his and barely stopped herself from moaning. This was strange on so many levels, but oh, wow, it was irresistible.

He ended the kiss and turned her loose, smiled and said, "See you." And then he was gone.

What just happened here?

A FEW DAYS after the fund-raiser Turner met his brother, Spencer, at the Last Stand Saloon for a beer and a pool game or two. Drinking a beer and sitting in the alcove that held the pool table, he waited for Spencer and tried to figure out his next step.

Since the fund-raiser at Jameson House, he'd been dreaming a lot. Hot dreams starring none other than Charlie Stockton. Not regular Charlie, the Charlie he was used to, either. Charlie in that killer red dress. That low-cut, curve-hugging, red formal dress. If getting her out of his mind had been difficult before, it was impossible now.

He'd caught Charlie by surprise when he'd kissed her. The way she'd responded had surprised *him*. That kiss had been even better than he'd imagined, and he'd bet his last dollar that she'd enjoyed it as much as he had. It had been damn hard to stop and even harder to pretend to a nonchalance he sure as hell didn't feel.

So what did he do now?

In the past, he'd thought about them becoming friends with benefits. But that wasn't what he wanted. Okay, of course he wanted the benefits, but he wanted more. He wanted to see where their relationship could go. Which he'd told her. And she acted as if she'd never even thought about it.

"Earth to Turner," he heard Spencer say. "Where were you? I said your name three times before you looked up. You're bound to have heard me. The jukebox isn't even playing." He set down his beer and picked up a pool cue to chalk it.

"I was thinking about a case," Turner said. He wasn't ready to admit that he'd been daydreaming about Charlie.

"Oh, really? Looked to me like you were thinking about a woman. The old *what the hell do I do now* expression."

"Rack 'em," he told Spencer and grabbed his own cue. They flipped a coin to see who broke. As usual with Spencer, Turner lost. His kid brother was one of the luckiest people he knew. Well, except for their sister Jessie, but she was a card shark. She didn't ordinarily play pool, but she whipped all their butts on the tenth of every month when they held family poker night at the McBride ranch.

Before he could decide how to answer, Spencer continued as he removed the rack and set up for his shot. "It wouldn't be Charlie you had on your mind, would it?"

"I didn't say I had a woman on my mind. Much less Charlie."

"Already told you, the look on your face telegraphed it." He broke and sank three balls, two solids and a striped. "Solids," he called and continued. "Besides, Graham bet me ten bucks that you'd be hitting on Charlie soon if you haven't already."

Turner snorted derisively. "Graham's got the hots for Bella. He thinks everyone should be like him."

"Graham said you looked gobsmacked at the fund-raiser Saturday night. And he didn't blame you. He said Charlie looked amazing." After sinking another two, Spencer missed.

"You two gossip like girls." But Graham was right. He had been gobsmacked. Turner proceeded to run the table. "Eight ball in the corner pocket." He sank it and told Spencer, "And that's how you do it."

"You know what they say. Lucky in pool, unlucky in love."

"The saying is lucky in cards."

Spencer lifted a shoulder. "Same principle."

They started another game. Turner wrestled with what to say. Wanting to change from friends to lovers was a whole new experience for him, and he wasn't sure how to approach it. Kissing Charlie had been a start. That should get her at least thinking about the two of them, especially since he'd hung that idea out there. But what the hell was he supposed to do now?

"Damn, Turner, you're doing it again. Spill."

Turner eyed his brother. Spencer never seemed to lack for women. Maybe he'd have an idea of what he should do next. "Have you ever tried to go from being friends to lovers?"

"With a woman?"

"I'm not gay, so yes, with a woman."

"With Charlie."

Turner simply nodded and missed a shot.

"The only woman I've ever been really good friends with is very happily married. So no. But what's the problem?"

"The problem is I'm not sure how to…get things going."

"Did you try kissing her?"

"Yes."

"Aha. Was it good?"

"Of course it was good. Why would I want to be more than friends otherwise? What a dumbass question."

"Hey, you're the one asking for my advice. Which is kind of funny, really, since I'm your younger brother. Now I just need Graham to come to me for advice on his love life, and I'll officially be the smart one in the family."

"More like smart-ass. I don't want your advice on my love life. I'm just trying to figure out where I go from here."

"Ask her out."

"I did. We went to the fund-raiser."

"Ask her out again. Romance her. You do know how to romance a woman, right?"

Turner gave him a dirty look. "What do you think?"

Spencer just grinned. "Treat her like you would any woman you're interested in. She's no different, except you ought to have a really good idea of what she likes."

True. He knew what flowers she liked. What music she liked. What movies she liked. He knew the kind of food she liked—and what she hated. He knew she had a soft spot for babies, both animal and human. He knew she'd moved to California to try to make it on to a televised cooking show competition. And she had, though she hadn't won. She'd married the man who won it. And later divorced him.

He didn't know why the marriage broke up. But he knew that she hadn't had a serious relationship since she came back to Last Stand. Was that because she hadn't wanted one? If so, it made sense that she'd dated Rick Wallace, since everyone knew his rep as a player. Or maybe she simply hadn't found the right guy.

Was he the right man for her? Was she the right woman for him? Turner couldn't say for certain, but he wanted the chance to find out. He already liked her more than any other woman he knew. Romance her, Spencer had told him. He could do that.

Chapter Three

CHAR-PIE, CHARLIE AND Audrey Stockton's pie shop, stood in one of the choice locations along Last Stand's Main Street, directly across from the library and in the next block over from the Carriage House restaurant.

Out front on the wooden sidewalk, there was a wooden bench with a planter of flowers on either end. On one side of the bright green doors was a small metal table and two chairs, also green. The building itself was native limestone, like so many buildings in the Texas Hill Country. A large plate-glass window displayed Char-Pie's wares, and the pie of the day was printed on an old-fashioned wooden chalkboard.

The doors opened into a surprisingly spacious shop, filled with wood-topped tables and colorful wooden chairs, along with a glass-fronted refrigerated display case filled with pies of every description, artistically arranged. Next to the showcase, a cash register sat on a long counter, with jars of homemade jams and jellies made by some of the locals. Charlie left the decor and staging up to her sister Audrey most of the time, as Audrey had a real talent for it. Charlie concentrated on the food. The atmosphere was homey and inviting, the pies were delicious, and the coffee always fresh and aromatic. Consequently, Char-Pie did a good business. The fact that two pretty women ran it didn't hurt business either. Or so she'd been told, surprisingly, mostly by their older clients.

Several days after the fund-raiser, Audrey was out front taking care of customers and Charlie was in the kitchen making lemon meringue pies. Which, since it was his favorite, made her think of Turner—as if she needed encouragement. She was still wondering how serious he was about the two of them becoming more than friends.

"Holy cow," Audrey said, coming into the kitchen. "You need to come out here right now. We just got a delivery." Charlie's sister was a redhead, with beautiful pale skin that really set off her hair. And unlike Charlie, who was at best medium height and not by any means thin, Audrey was tall and slim. If Audrey hadn't been her sister, Charlie might have hated her.

"It will have to wait a minute. Let me get these pies in the oven and then I'll come. What is it?"

"You have to see it to believe it. Hurry up." She disappeared through the kitchen doorway.

A few minutes later, Charlie went out front. "What the heck?" A huge vase of flowers stood on the counter. "Who are they for?"

"They're for you."

"For me? Who would send me flowers?"

"I've been trying to figure that out. Rick Wallace, maybe. Trying to make up with you. I didn't read the card," Audrey said virtuously. "But it was a close thing."

Peonies. A huge vase of at least two dozen peonies ranging in color from the palest pink to crimson. Her favorite flower in the world. Somehow she couldn't see Rick going to this amount of trouble. He'd undoubtedly already moved on, which was fine with her.

She buried her nose in the blooms, inhaling the sweet, almost intoxicating scent. "Who could have sent these?"

"Open up the card," Audrey commanded. "I'm dying to know."

Charlie's heart beat faster. She plucked the card from its holder. She knew that handwriting. But... She opened the card, elbowing aside her sister who was trying to read over her shoulder. *Have dinner with me tonight. Carriage House. Seven thirty. I'll buy you a steak.* There was no signature, but she knew who had written it.

Turner.

"There's no signature," Audrey said, snatching the card out of her suddenly nerveless fingers. "Who is it?" She looked from the card to Charlie. "You know who it is, don't you?"

"I think so." No, she knew so.

"Who? You're making me crazy. Tell me who sent them."

"Turner."

"Turner McBride?"

Charlie nodded.

"Something happened at the fund-raiser, didn't it? Tell me," she demanded.

"Nothing happened."

"Girl, you are a terrible liar."

That was true. She worried her lip, wondering if she should tell her sister what was going on. Audrey would take it as a sign, since she'd thought Charlie and Turner should have gotten together years ago. Still, she knew she'd wind up telling her, so she might as well tell Audrey now than later. "It wasn't what I expected. Turner asked me if I'd ever thought about becoming more than friends." Audrey's eyes widened so she added, "And he wasn't just talking about hooking up."

"So now he's sending you gorgeous flowers?" Audrey whooped. "It's about time. I've been waiting for this for ages."

"Waiting for what? He's one of my oldest friends."

"Yeah. One of your oldest and *hottest* friends." Audrey clapped her hands and sighed. "This is great."

The bells above the door jingled and a customer entered. Audrey went to help them after telling Charlie she'd be back.

Audrey took care of the customer in record time. "All right, what else happened at the fund-raiser? Or afterward?" Audrey stared at her for a long moment. "You slept together!"

Charlie flushed, wishing the thought didn't send a shiver of excitement up her spine. "Of course we didn't."

"Something happened."

"He kissed me. When he took me home."

"So? Is that a big deal?"

Charlie didn't answer.

"You mean you've really never kissed Turner before?"

"Only the one time I told you about, when we were teenagers."

"All that hotness and you never even kissed properly?"

"I told you, we're friends."

"Oh, honey. This—" she waved a hand at the flowers "—this is not about friendship. He has the hots for you. It's totally obvious."

"No he doesn't."

Then what would you call it?

I have no idea.

"Why are you so reluctant?"

"Because we're friends and I don't want to screw that up. Turner's friendship is important to me. And if we dated…" She shook her head. "It's not worth the risk."

"Speak of the devil," Audrey said mischievously. "Look who just walked in. Hi, Turner. Don't mind me. I'm just going to check on a pie."

Charlie grabbed hold of her shirt and whispered sharply, "Don't you dare leave."

Audrey simply laughed and left her.

"Hi," Turner said. "I see you got the flowers."

"Yes. Thank you. They're beautiful. But why did you send them?"

"Because peonies are your favorite."

Yes, they were. But that didn't answer her question. "Is this part of your plan for us to start dating?"

"It's because I wanted to give you flowers. Are you going to the Carriage House with me tonight?"

She supposed that was the closest she'd get to an answer.

"I don't know."

"I'll buy you a steak. That's your favorite, isn't it?"

"You know it is."

"Then how about it?"

"I don't think you've thought this through. This—" she motioned between them "—this you and me thing."

He smiled at her. The smile that brought out his dimples. The one he usually reserved for women he was hitting on. Or wanted to hit on.

"You're wrong there, Charlie. I've thought about it a lot."

"We're friends. Friends don't date."

"Sure they do. Look, you're not dating anyone, right?"

She shrugged. "Right."

"And I'm not dating anyone. So why shouldn't we spend some time together? Why shouldn't we explore our options?"

Explore their options. If she had any sense she'd tell him no. "All right. I'll meet you there at seven thirty."

"Great. Can I get a piece of lemon meringue pie to go?"

"Of course." She boxed up his pie thinking, *Obviously, I have no sense. No sense at all.*

༝

CHARLIE LOVED THE Carriage House. It was an institution in Last Stand, the original building having been around since the days of horses and buggies. But the thing she really loved was their steak. Which Turner knew and had used to bribe her with.

Charlie arrived a little late. "Hi, Rhonda," she said, greeting the hostess. "I'm meeting Turner for dinner. Is he here yet?"

"Hi, Charlie. He sure is. Let me take you to him."

Rhonda led her through the ground-floor dining room to the circular iron staircase with wooden steps. The main dining room of the restaurant retained a good bit of the original structure, with a high vaulted ceiling and dark wood beams and a gleaming hardwood floor. The room was filled with cozy booths along the edges and tables with white tablecloths throughout. There was a wonderful mahogany bar that was a favorite meeting place for Charlie and her friends to have drinks, unless they met at the Saloon, another fixture in Last Stand, though it was more casual.

Turner had chosen a table on the second floor, which was well known for its romantic ambience. Charlie had eaten upstairs a couple of times before, both times with men who were trying to impress her. And now Turner. He was pulling out all the stops.

"So, you and Turner, huh?" Rhonda said on the way up the stairs. "It's about time you two got together."

"What? No, no. We're just friends." And she was determined to stay that way. Steamy kiss or not.

"If you say so, honey. Here we are."

Turner stood and pulled her chair out for her. He wore khakis and a button-down long-sleeved baby-blue dress shirt and he looked good. Really good. Damn it.

"Have fun, you two," Rhonda said, winking and handing her a menu. "Your server will be here in a moment."

"I was beginning to worry that you weren't coming. You look fantastic, by the way."

"Why wouldn't I come?" she asked, ignoring his comment about how she looked. She wore a bright blue fitted sleeveless shift, shirred at the waist, with big dangly earrings and matching blue high-heeled sandals. She knew she looked nice, but fantastic? Not hardly.

"I don't know. You're late and you're never late."

"Well, I was this time." Their waiter came and took their drink orders—a glass of red wine for both of them. Charlie wanted to probe further into Turner's intentions, but he started talking about work, his and hers, asking her about how the shop was doing and telling her a funny story about life at the hospital. Pretty soon they were talking like they always did.

Their dinner arrived, delicious as usual. After that they sat talking for quite a while, about Last Stand happenings, movies, books and whatever else came to mind. Just like they always did, they never lacked for something to talk about. Maybe he'd changed his mind. Maybe he hadn't meant it. He'd only been teasing.

And why that thought should depress her when she knew it would be better for the two of them to avoid dating, she didn't know.

After they left the Carriage House, Turner insisted on walking her to her car, so she didn't argue. She'd parked on the street, a couple of blocks down from the restaurant. The night was cool for a change and for once the humidity wasn't bad. "I had a nice time tonight, Turner. Thanks for dinner."

"I had a good time too. But I always do with you. Here's my car. I need to get something out of it."

She stopped while he retrieved a pretty, wrapped rectangular package from his car. "What's that?" she asked.

"You'll see," he said, tucking it under his arm.

When they reached her car and she opened the door, Turner handed her the package. "I saw this and thought of you."

"You got me a present?"

"It's not a big deal."

"Why did you get me a present?"

"I told you. I saw it and thought you'd like it. Open it."

"The paper is so pretty, I hate to mess it up." Carefully, she unwrapped it, doing her best not to tear it. She sensed Turner becoming impatient and when he spoke he confirmed it.

"Just rip the damn paper," he said.

She gave him a reproving look and continued carefully opening it. As she'd figured, it was a book—a hardback edition of one of her favorite Nora Roberts books. Opening it she realized it was a signed first edition. She looked up from the book to see Turner smiling at her, though a little anxiously.

"This is—Wow, Turner. How did you know I love her books?"

Turner laughed. "Please. Anyone who's been in your house can look at your bookcases and see that she's one of your favorites. I know you've probably read it, but I thought you might get a kick out of a signed first edition."

"You thought right. Thank you. It's wonderful. And very thoughtful." She narrowed her eyes at him. "You still think we should date, don't you?"

"Yes. Why would I have changed my mind?"

"Because you thought better of it. We're friends. You know if we get involved romantically we risk losing what we have."

"I don't see why. If things don't work out, we'll go back to being friends."

"It won't be that easy."

"How do you know? Have you ever tried it with anyone else?"

"No, but everyone says—"

Turner laughed. "Since when do you pay attention to what *everyone* says?" He drew his finger down her nose. "Besides, there's too much between us. We could never not be friends. Take care. I'll see you soon." And he walked away.

Charlie knew what was going on. Turner was trying to drive her crazy. And he was succeeding. Given the subject of their conversation, she'd thought he'd kiss her. But he hadn't. For this very reason—so that she'd continue to think about him long after they parted.

A signed first edition of an extremely popular author's book wasn't something you bought on a whim. Turner had put some thought into it. So it wasn't the gift that impressed her as much as the thought behind it. God, she was a sucker. A sucker for a romantic gesture.

A sucker for Turner McBride.

TURNER DIDN'T SEE Charlie for a couple of weeks after their dinner at the Carriage House, though he talked to her on the phone several times. Work kept him busy. He had several long and involved cases, more than he usually did. He worked Memorial Day weekend, then later in the week traveled to Dallas to give a lecture at Southwestern Medical School. Rather than trying to make it in one day, which would have made for a very long one, he stayed overnight.

Like almost everyone in the hospital, he'd been invited to Emily Prior's wedding and reception. She was the chief of surgery's daughter and only child, and the reception promised to be a blowout. It was the perfect chance to take Charlie out again. Not to mention, there was supposed to be a killer band at the reception and he knew Charlie loved to dance.

He dropped by the pie shop shortly before closing. Both Audrey and Charlie were busy serving people, so he hung back, sitting down at one of the tables with a copy of *The Defender*, Last Stand's local newspaper. Eventually the last customer left and Turner tucked the paper under his arm and ambled over to the counter. "Got any key lime pie left?" he asked.

Charlie had stayed out front while Audrey disappeared into the kitchen. "I saw you come in but I thought you'd left. No key lime. No lemon meringue either. But we have peach cobbler."

"I'll take a piece."

"Technically we're closed, you know," she told him as she cut a generous piece of cobbler.

He nodded. "I know. I saw you turn the sign around." He put down the paper and began to eat standing at the counter. "This is really good. I should get cobbler more often."

"Is that all, Turner? I have a bunch of things to do."

"It's not. How about being my plus-one at Emily Prior's wedding and reception this weekend?"

"You're going to a wedding? Voluntarily?"

"She's the chief of surgery's daughter, so it's pretty much a command performance. But I've heard they have a really good band booked for the reception."

"Who?"

He named a fairly well-known country-western band from Austin. "I'll even promise to dance with you all you want."

"I thought you hated to dance. You must really be hard up for a date."

"I'm not hard up. It's you or no one. And I don't hate to dance."

"News to me." She looked at him a moment. "If I say I'll go, it's not a date."

"What's wrong with having a date?"

"You and I are friends. Friends don't date."

Oh, yes, they do, he thought, hiding a smile. "Fine. It's not a date. We'll just hang out together at the wedding and reception." Of course it was a date. But if it made her happy to pretend it wasn't, that was okay with him.

"And dance. Don't forget that."

"Wouldn't dream of it."

Charlie's younger sister, Audrey, poked her head out the kitchen door. "I can't find the new paddle. Where did you put it?"

"Beside the ovens, where I always keep them."

"Hi, Turner," Audrey said. "I wondered who Charlie was talking to."

Turner smiled at her. "Hi, Audrey." Audrey was a tall, beautiful redhead, but Turner only had eyes for one Stockton sister. "I'm trying to convince your sister to go to a wedding with me this weekend."

"Emily Prior's wedding?" Turner nodded. "You should go, Charlie. I hear they're having a great band at the reception."

"I can arrange my own dates," Charlie said dryly.

"You just said it wasn't a date," Turner pointed out. "Did you change your mind?"

Audrey laughed and disappeared back into the kitchen.

Charlie scowled at Turner. "No. I misspoke. You need to go now, Turner. I have things to do before I can go home."

"You haven't said you'd go with me."

She rolled her eyes. "Fine. I'll go, but on one condition."

"It's not a date?" he guessed.

"Right."

"Okay, I'll pick you up at six thirty for our non-date." He handed her the empty plate. "Thanks for the pie." He pulled some money out of his pocket but she stopped him before he could toss it down.

"It's after hours. You don't need to pay for the pie."

He smiled. "I'll have to remember that."

"It's a one-time thing."

He laughed and left the shop.

Chapter Four

*W*HY DID *I say I'd go to a wedding with Turner? Weddings make me sentimental.* Not even the end of her marriage had made her dislike weddings. She still thought they were so romantic. Which Turner, the sneaky devil, undoubtedly remembered.

The couple were young and obviously in love. The bride was exquisite in her white wedding gown with a beaded bodice, full skirt, and a long lace train. If the look on his face when he saw her was anything to go by, the groom was clearly head over heels for his bride.

The church was beautiful, with flowers everywhere. She sneaked a glance at Turner. Damn, she'd seen him in a suit before—and in a tux as well—but tonight he looked well, gorgeous. The navy suit with the baby-blue dress shirt fit him to perfection. The beautiful silk tie in shades of blue with a pinstripe of red accented the suit perfectly. He wore a lot of blue, which intensified the color of his blue eyes and made them even prettier. He could have been a model or a movie star rather than a dedicated neurosurgeon. And how did he manage to look as mouth-watering in jeans and a T-shirt as he did in this suit? He even looked good in scrubs.

It's so not fair.

And what the hell was she doing thinking of Turner in those terms? Friend, she reminded herself. Just a friend.

Naturally, he caught her looking at him and gave her a slow, sexy smile. Irked as much by her own reaction as his, she leaned closer and asked, "Does that work on all the women?"

He laughed. "I never thought about it. Is it working on you?"

She shook her head. "Sorry. It doesn't do a thing for me." But of course, it did. It kind of made her stomach flutter. *Kind of? Right.*

Luckily the music was loud at the moment, so it covered up their discussion. Charlie congratulated herself on managing to make it through the ceremony without crying.

The reception was held at Dr. Prior's country club. It was everything it had been rumored to be. Great food, free booze, and a smokin' hot band. They were more country rock than plain country-western, and it made them even more fun to dance to. True to his word, Turner danced with her almost every song.

"This is nice," she said during a slow song. He had his arm around her holding her close but not too close, her head lay against his chest, her hand was tucked in his, the music was a sweet, haunting melody, and she'd had just enough champagne to relax her and make her not worry about a thing.

"More than nice," he said, his voice a deep rumble.

She glanced up at him to see him looking at her with an

intense expression in his eyes. "Perfect," he said, and added, "Almost."

Charlie's breath caught in her throat. The way he was looking at her had her stomach tumbling and the rest of her tingling. *Uh-oh.* "Isn't that a movie?"

Turner laughed. "No. You're thinking of *Almost Famous.*"

Whew. That was close. "I'm thirsty. Will you go get me a drink?"

"Sure. Alcoholic or non?"

She should go with non. But one more drink wouldn't hurt, would it? "Champagne. I never have champagne." He turned her loose and she went to their table. So what if it was her third glass when she rarely had more than one or at most two? She was tired of being cautious. Besides, she didn't have work tomorrow, so she could afford to indulge.

"Looking good," she heard a male voice say.

She turned her head and saw Rick Wallace. Speaking of looking good, there was no denying he was. She'd had fun with him while it lasted. Mostly. Their breakup had been mutual. Again, mostly. Enough so that they'd parted amicably and she considered him a friend. Sometimes she wondered if Rick might have been interested in taking the relationship further, but while she liked Rick, she couldn't imagine getting involved with him for more than a short period of time. "Thanks." She knew the pale peach sleeveless dress with its V-neck, fitted top and flared skirt looked good on her but it was nice to have that reaffirmed by two different men.

Rick sat down and began flirting with her. Not surprising. His go-to with a woman—any woman—was to flirt. He hadn't been there long when Turner came back with their drinks. He and Rick greeted each other as he set her glass in front of her.

"How about a dance?" Rick asked Charlie. "Come on, for old time's sake."

Before she could respond Turner said, "She can't. She's dancing with me."

"Doesn't look like it," Rick said.

"Don't be a douche, Rick," Turner said, and hustled Charlie out to the dance floor.

"What is wrong with you? I can't believe you called him a douche. I thought you two were friends?"

"We are. When he's not being a douchebag and trying to get rid of me so he can hit on you." The song changed to a slow ballad. Turner pulled her closer and said, "I don't want to talk about him anymore. Forget about him and we'll just enjoy the party."

They danced. Slow songs, fast songs and everything in between. When the band took a break Turner said, "Let's take a walk."

She didn't argue, but let him take her hand and lead her outside. They strolled around the grounds near the clubhouse. Low standing lights illuminated the pathways, both so they could see their way and see the flowers and shrubs as well. They weren't the only people strolling around outside, but Charlie felt as if they were. Turner held her hand as they walked the path until he found an empty bench and they sat down.

She was alone in the moonlight with a man she'd thought she knew inside and out. But she didn't know *this* Turner, the man romancing her. The man who made her want and made her question every decision she thought she'd made. Turner was a man who focused on his objective and didn't let anything get in his way. She knew what it had taken for him to get through medical school and residency, to go even further and become a neurosurgeon. But Turner had known what he wanted and gone after it. *Nothing* had stopped him.

Now he'd apparently decided he wanted her. And it wasn't a whim. Turner was doing a great job tempting her to forget caution. Forget about the possibility of ruining their friendship if this thing between them should fail.

He held her hand, his thumb tracing patterns on her palm. "What are you thinking about?"

She looked at him, at the face she knew so well. She knew what he looked like when he was happy, when he was sad, when he was angry or hurt or impatient. She'd seen him in doctor mode, seen his single-minded determination to do the best that he could for his patients.

She'd seen him in love—but never in love with her. "I thought I knew you so well. But I don't. I've never seen this side of you."

"You do know me." He brought her hand to his lips and kissed it. "You know me better than anyone does, except possibly my family. What side have you never seen?"

"You're romancing me, aren't you." It wasn't a question.

She knew the answer.

A slow smile curved his mouth. "Yes. Is that a bad thing?"

She shook her head. "No. But it's confusing."

"Because you don't know what you want?"

"I know what I want," she said and watched his eyes darken. "But I don't know what is right for us."

He leaned forward and kissed her. Soft, sweet but with more than a hint of desire. Charlie let herself go with it, questions and doubts cast aside. Only their lips touched, and their hands where he held hers.

He ended the kiss, but slowly. "I'll help you figure it out.

AFTER THE RECEPTION Turner drove Charlie home and parked in her driveway. Knowing she wouldn't be in a long dress since the wedding wasn't formal, he'd brought his Corvette again. "Can I ask you something?" he said before she could open her door.

"Okay." Sounding wary, she settled back in the seat.

"Why did you and Wallace break up?"

"Why do you want to know?"

"I don't want to make the same mistakes he made. You don't have to answer. But you two are still friends and it's plain he isn't over you."

"Rick always flirts. It doesn't mean anything."

"What if it does?"

The porch light shone through the window, softly illuminating her face. She shook her head. "Rick knew from the start that we were only having fun. It was never meant to be serious. Besides, you know his reputation. He's a player. He never sticks with one woman for long."

"But you were different. He changed his mind, didn't he?"

She was quiet for a long moment. "I don't know," she said slowly. "I was afraid he had. I probably imagined it, though."

"I don't think so. He wants you back."

"Because he flirts with me?"

"That. And because of the way he looks at you. He's not over you," Turner repeated.

"You're wrong. And it wouldn't matter anyway. We're over and he knows that."

"Why are you so adamant about not getting serious, Charlie?"

"I'm divorced. Isn't that reason enough?"

"I don't know. Is it?"

She didn't answer.

"I know a lot of things about you but there's one facet of your life I know very little about."

"My marriage and divorce."

He nodded. "You've never said much beyond he wasn't who you thought he was when you married him."

"I believe I also said he was a stinking bastard."

"You did. But that's all you said."

"I can't talk about it, Turner."

He searched her face for a moment, then said, "Then we

won't."

She got out and walked around to the back door, unlocked it and went inside. Turner followed. She tossed her purse on the counter, kicked off her shoes and walked into the living room. Again, he followed.

"Are you mad at me?" she asked him.

"No. Why would I be?"

"Because I can't talk about my marriage. I know I should but I—"

He closed the gap between them and laid his fingers against her mouth. "Don't apologize. Whether you tell me about it now, or later, or never at all is completely your choice. I would never be mad at you for that." He dropped his hand, though he wanted to run his fingers over her soft lips.

"Thank you. You're a good friend." Her eyes were bright with unshed tears. The very last thing Turner wanted was to make her cry.

"I'm an even better lover."

As he'd intended, the comment made her smile. "I have no doubt."

"Since this wasn't a date I suppose a good-night kiss is out of the question."

This time she laughed. "I'll concede this was a date. And a good-night kiss is very much in play." Her lipstick was gone but her lips looked plump and inviting. He slipped his arms around her, bent his head down and kissed her. Her lips opened and her arms crept up around his neck. He took the invitation and touched his tongue to hers. She answered immediately, her breasts crushed against his chest, her tongue dueling with his in a sexy dance of pleasure. He shot into overdrive in five seconds flat. He wanted to feel her soft bare skin against his. Wanted to kiss and caress her breasts, wanted to back her up against the door, push up her dress and strip off her panties. Wanted to—

What the hell are you doing? It's a good-night kiss. Not a prelude to hot, blow-the-top-of-your-head-off sex.

Except he couldn't remember ever getting so hot, so fast. And sure as hell not from a simple kiss. He lifted his head and stared at her, aware that she was breathing as heavily as he was. It took all of his willpower to let her go instead of kissing her again and seeing where it led. But he knew exactly where it would lead. To Charlie's bed. And while her body might be all for it, he was damn sure her mind was not.

She was staring at him, looking as dazed as he felt. "I'll call you." He walked out her door before he blew every one of his good resolutions to hell and back.

CHARLIE MET HER sister at the shop Sunday afternoon to get ready for work Monday morning. The moment she saw her, Audrey said, "How was the wedding?"

Charlie got out the ingredients for making her grandmother's secret pie dough recipe. Pastry flour, butter, shortening, salt, and the secret ingredient, vinegar. Charlie had promised to only share the recipe with family. The key, she'd found, was how the crust was put together. It had taken her a while to figure out how to make a large batch of it. The dough didn't keep forever, but would last a few days in the refrigerator.

While she worked she said, "I told you what happened at the fund-raiser."

Audrey was working on a new display for the front window, so she was going in and out of the kitchen. "You said he wants to date you."

"He does. And stupidly, I agreed to go with him to that wedding and reception."

Audrey disappeared and reappeared. "Why is that stupid?"

"Because now he's romancing me. Oh, hell, he's been doing that from the first. The flowers, the dinner, the book—"

"What book?"

"I thought I told you. After our dinner at the Carriage House, he gave me a signed first edition of one of my favorite author's books."

"I'm sure you flipped over it."

"Pretty much. It showed how well he knows me."

"He should. You've known each other since you were twelve or thirteen." She changed the subject. "Come see the display."

"I'll be there in a minute." She finished making the dough, covered it and put it in the refrigerator, then followed her sister out front.

"I like it," she said when she saw the display. It was simple but very cute. The pie of the day was posted on an old-fashioned blackboard slate. In front of it was a display pie. A doll made to look like a baker with a chef's hat was placed beside it. Next to that, in the middle of the window, was a picnic basket on a red checked tablecloth, another pie and a bottle of wine. There was a saying printed on a place card that read: *A bottle of wine, an apple pie, and you. What more could you ask for?*

"Where is that quote from? I never can remember."

"It's a paraphrase of something Omar Khayyam said in *The Rubaiyat.*"

"How do you know these things?" Charlie asked, momentarily diverted.

"You forget, I majored in literature."

"Oh, yeah. Well, it comes in handy sometimes."

Audrey laughed. "I guess it does. Okay, what happened at the wedding reception?"

"We danced. A lot. Rick tried to dance with me and Turner called him a douche. Again. But to his face this time."

Audrey let out a peal of laughter. "Poor Rick. He's probably getting a complex."

"Hmph. I doubt that. Anyway, we went for a walk around the grounds and sat on a bench and talked. And then he kissed me in the moonlight." She sighed heavily. "It doesn't sound like much when I say it out loud, but it really was romantic."

Audrey blinked at her. "It sounds romantic to me. Did he kiss you again after that? Did you sleep together?"

"What is with you? No, I didn't sleep with him. I'm still

not even sure about us dating, much less having sex. But I have to admit he's tempting. When he kissed me good night…" She closed her eyes, reliving that moment. "Oh, my God, Audrey, it was hot. Super hot."

"Like make you want to strip off your panties hot?"

Charlie laughed. "Pretty much."

Audrey sighed. "I don't see what the problem is. Other than he's got you in a tizzy."

"I'm not in a tizzy." The timer dinged and Charlie got up to take pies out of the oven and move them to the cooling rack. "I don't want to ruin our friendship. And I'm not interested in getting involved with anyone."

"Which is why you dated Rick Wallace. Because you knew he wouldn't get serious. And neither would you."

"Right. And you know why." She liked Rick. He was a player, but he was also a nice guy. Charlie admitted that one of the things that had made him so attractive to her was that she knew he wouldn't expect more than she could give.

"It's different with Turner," Audrey commented. "You're afraid you could get serious with him."

Why deny it? "Yes."

"Why do you need to worry about that now? Why can't you just take each day as it comes and enjoy yourself?"

"What if we do start dating? What if we fall in love? Turner is a traditional guy. He's a family kind of guy."

"So? Again, what's the problem?"

"You know what it is. The reason why my marriage failed."

"Charlie, you have to stop blaming yourself for that.

Your marriage failed because your ex is a selfish prick. Not because you had to have a hysterectomy."

Hindsight. If only she'd had a child when she wanted to. If she hadn't listened to Lance, if she hadn't put it off, she might never have developed the endometriosis that forced her to have a hysterectomy. "It doesn't matter. I still can't ever give Turner a child of his own."

"But you don't know if that matters to him."

"No, I don't. And maybe he won't care now. I'm sure he'd say he doesn't. But he will. At some point, he will want children of his own. And once was enough to go through that particular hell." Her dreams of having a baby had died with her hysterectomy, her marriage shortly after that. Having her husband tell her he'd changed his mind and wanted a child of his own, when he'd sworn he didn't and even refused to try had sent her reeling. Especially coming so soon after the hysterectomy. So when he asked for a divorce, she hadn't fought him. There was no way she wanted a man who didn't want her. Or a man who would walk out on her when she was at the lowest point in her life.

So she'd come home and picked up the pieces of her life. She was happy now, with her sister and her friends, and her business. And she did love Last Stand. But she couldn't deny she had regrets. The biggest being that she'd never have a child of her own, and she didn't believe there was a man out there who wouldn't be—at the least—disappointed when he found out. Not even Turner.

Chapter Five

A FEW DAYS after the wedding, Turner decided to surprise Charlie at home. He chose a Thursday night because he was 90 percent sure she would be home. And if she had a date…well, he'd cross that bridge if and when he came to it. Thankfully, there was no car in front of her house, so if she was there, she'd be alone. He rang her doorbell around eight, armed with a gallon of cookies and cream ice cream—Charlie's favorite, of course. According to Charlie, the best movies were those from the eighties to the early 2000s, so he chose an old chick flick he knew she liked, *How to Lose A Guy in 10 Days*. Personally, he thought it looked kinda dumb, but he hadn't gotten it for himself. He'd bought her a DVD instead of trying to stream it. He knew she liked to have the DVD in hand since she didn't trust streaming services not to pull the rug out from under her. Or e-books either, for that matter.

Charlie opened the door. "Turner? What are you doing here?"

"Hi, I come bearing gifts." He held out the ice cream first and she took it from him.

Her hair was piled on the top of her head with a clip,

and stuck out every which way. She'd taken off her makeup and wore her pajamas—plaid cotton flannel pants and a T-shirt that said, "Pie Makes It All Better," with a picture of a pie in the middle. She looked cute. Very cute. He liked that.

Charlie stood there awhile, holding the ice cream and just staring at him.

"Are you going to let me in? And you might want to put that in the freezer if we're not going to eat it right away."

She stood aside and closed the door after him. "We?"

"Hey, I like ice cream, too."

She shook her head and took the ice cream to the kitchen where she got out two bowls and spoons. She opened another drawer and got out an ice cream scoop. The utensils were lined up with military precision. "Are all your drawers like that?"

"Like what? Organized?"

"Ruthlessly organized. It's like the utensils wouldn't dare be out of place."

"What do you expect? I'm a baker. I need to know where everything is. Besides, you're one to talk. I've seen your drawers."

She had a point, although he didn't think his drawers were quite as organized as hers.

Charlie finished scooping the ice cream and handed him a bowl. "We can eat in the den. I take it that's a movie in your hand."

"It is."

Charlie put away the ice cream and picked up her bowl to take with her, spooning a bite into her mouth first.

"Yum."

"You'll like the movie too," he said.

"Not if it's one of those gory action flicks you like so much."

"Oh, ye of little faith. Would I bring over a movie you'd hate?"

"Yes." She started naming several movies he'd talked her into seeing, most of which she'd hated.

Turner held up a hand. "This is a chick flick. At least, I think it is."

She sat on the couch. "You're kidding. And you're sticking around to watch it?"

"I'm broadening my horizons. I'll go put it on." He set down his ice cream and went over to her entertainment area.

"What's the name of the movie?"

"You'll see."

"I'm not apologizing for the way I look."

He looked at her over his shoulder. "Why would you? You look cute." He turned on the DVD player and picked up the remote. "I'll even let you have the controls."

"Who are you and what have you done with Turner McBride?"

He laughed and sat beside her. "Do you mind if I take off my shoes?" he asked her.

"I'm in my pajamas. What do you think?"

He took off his shoes and got comfortable, sitting close to Charlie but not close enough to crowd her.

The movie came on and Charlie turned and stared at him with her mouth open. "*How to Lose a Guy in 10 Days* is one of my favorite movies. And last I heard, you swore you'd never watch it."

"Changed my mind," he said, spooning ice cream into his mouth.

"Why?"

"Why not?"

She just shook her head and settled back to watch. To Turner's complete surprise, he enjoyed the movie. It was light-hearted and funny, ridiculous but in an amusing way. He liked watching Charlie's reactions to it. By the end of it, she was snuggled up against his side and he had his arm around her. He had to work to keep his hand at her waist and not caress the curves he knew were beneath the pajamas.

When the movie was over, Charlie asked, "Well, what did you think?"

"Surprisingly funny. I liked it."

"Careful. Next thing we know you'll be losing your manliness."

"My manliness is just fine. It can handle an occasional chick flick."

"Glad to hear it." She smiled and scooted away from him. "Thanks for bringing the movie. And for the ice cream."

He stood and so did she. "I should get going. It's getting late."

She walked him to the door and put her hand on his arm. "Tonight was very sweet and thoughtful of you." Then she rose on her toes and kissed him.

It was the first time she'd initiated a kiss. He slipped an

arm around her, careful not to push, to let her set the pace. Her tongue slid inside his mouth and touched his. They did a little dance of give and take and it started to heat up. Charlie ended it, gave him a sweet smile and he walked out the door.

He'd fallen for her. Hard.

FOR THE NEXT week, Charlie saw Turner almost every day. He came to her shop or dropped by her house with thoughtful gifts. He gave her wildflowers. He brought her favorite candy and stayed to eat it with her. He brought her more books—paperbacks, hardbacks, he even gifted her with e-books. Anything he thought she might like. He gave her odd knickknacks. Kitchen utensils she didn't have the heart to tell him she already had. Decorative items like Texas memorabilia. He gave her a mug with a picture of a pie. Underneath that it said, "Stress cannot exist in the presence of pie." He gave her a T-shirt with a picture of a pie and the saying, "Whatever the question, pie is the answer."

One day near closing time, Turner came into the shop lugging a stuffed St. Bernard that was almost as big as he was. "Turner, what in the world are you doing?"

He plopped the dog on the counter. "I remembered you love stuffed animals and that you told me once you always wanted one of these great big ones. So, happy stuffed animal day."

"Is there a stuffed animal day?" Charlie asked, momentarily diverted.

"I have no idea, but if not there should be."

My Lord, it was big. And adorable. The pink tongue lolled from the creature's mouth at an angle. "It's very sweet of you but you really don't need to keep bringing me presents."

"Don't you like them?"

"Of course I like them. Who wouldn't? But that isn't the point."

"Seems like it is to me."

The bell over the door jangled and Josie Vance and Cal Ramsey entered the shop.

"Oh, thank goodness," Josie said, straightening the hem of her gray T-shirt with "Rough Hollow Farm and Orchards" stenciled across the front. "We were afraid you'd be closed already."

"Hi, y'all," Charlie said. "No, it's still fifteen minutes until closing. But even if I had been closed, for you two I'd have opened up again." Josie and Cal were regulars who, when they were in town, came in several times a week.

"I haven't seen you in a while, Cal. Is Oakland keeping you busy?" Charlie asked. Cal, a major league baseball player, had been picked up by Oakland a few weeks ago. Both he and Josie lived in California much of the time, but all the Ramsey men were born and bred here, so they came home whenever they could. Josie was in Last Stand fairly often, but Cal couldn't get away as much with the season in full swing.

"We're just in town for a few days," Josie said. "We've been house hunting for a permanent place here," she added, looking at Cal with a soft smile. "Not that we don't love staying at the farm."

Turner and Cal shook hands. "I saw your left fielder pulled a hamstring the other night," Turner said. "What does that mean for you?"

"If I'm lucky, I'll get to start for the next few games."

"Hey, that's great, man. You've been hitting well when you're in the lineup. Hope it works out for you."

"Do you want your regular?" Charlie asked. "Coconut cream for you," she said to Josie. "And French silk for you, Cal?"

"The perks of being a regular. Sounds great," Cal said. "The pie is not the same on the West Coast, by the way. I need my fix."

Josie had been eyeing the gigantic stuffed animal. "Your guard dog there is kind of intimidating."

Turner laughed. "He won't bite. I promise."

Charlie put their pie slices on plates and poured coffee for everyone while she listened to Turner and Cal talk baseball. Figuring Turner would want a piece too, she served him a slice of his favorite lemon meringue. The two men took their pie to a table and sat, leaving Josie and Charlie to chat at the counter. "Don't you want to sit down?" she asked Josie.

"No, I'm good." She forked a bite into her mouth and sighed happily. "This pie isn't going to last long anyway. It's delicious, as always." Josie nodded her head at the dog. "From Turner, I gather?"

"Yes. He knows I have a thing about stuffed animals. It's

a little over the top, but..." She shrugged.

"I think it's really sweet."

"He is sweet. He's been doing stuff like this for weeks now. Damn it," she added.

"Why damn it?" Josie asked with a quizzical expression.

"I'm trying to resist him and doing a crappy job of it." She remembered the night he'd brought over the movie and ice cream. Remembered kissing him before he left. Now why hadn't he kissed her since? Because he knew that would make her think about him that much more? Oh, he was sneaky. She wasn't sure how much longer she could hold out, even though she still had major concerns about what sex would do to their friendship. But sometimes, like when they kissed, she didn't care.

"Wow, where did you go, Charlie?" Josie asked her.

Charlie blushed. "Uh, nowhere."

Josie laughed and shook her head, dark curls bouncing. "Never mind. I think I know. You and Turner have known each other a long time, haven't you?"

"We've been friends since we were teenagers, yes. But we never dated or anything."

"Until now," Josie said.

"We've been out a few times. Not officially dating." No, she was just seeing him almost daily. But not dating. Not really.

Josie looked surprised. "Oh? So you're seeing other people?"

"Well, no. We hang out a lot. I mean, I see him almost every day, and I talk to him a lot even when I don't see him, but…" Her voice trailed off. Josie was very obviously struggling not to laugh. "Oh, hell. We are dating. Officially or exclusively or whatever you want to call it."

Josie did laugh now.

"How did you know? Is it that obvious?"

"The enormous dog was a hint, but honestly, it's how you look at each other."

"How we look at each other?"

"You've got some pretty heated glances going on."

"You're one to talk. I thought there was a heat wave when you two came in."

"It's July," Josie said. "I know I'm not a native, but I would bet there's always a heat wave in July in Last Stand."

"You have a point." She looked at the men, who'd already finished their pie and were talking earnestly. Undoubtedly about baseball.

Josie and Cal left soon after, saying they had more house hunting to do.

Charlie put the Closed sign up and said to Turner, "Something tells me wedding bells might be ringing soon."

"Yeah, house hunting together is a big clue."

"So was the way they looked at each other," Charlie said, thinking about what Josie had said. "Where do you want to eat?" Definitely time to change the subject.

"How about Hilde's Haus?" Turner asked, mentioning the diner on Main Street.

"Perfect. I still have a few things to do but it shouldn't take long." She'd had some free time earlier and had made piecrust to keep in the refrigerator until she needed it. She'd also prepared some of the fillings so that she could put together several pies first thing in the morning and cook them.

Turner had followed her into the kitchen and begun rinsing off dishes before putting them in the dishwasher.

"You don't need to do that, Turner." Although it did make her smile to think of Turner, a highly skilled neurosurgeon, doing something so domestic.

"It's not a problem. I do it all the time at the ranch." He paused and added, "When it's my turn, anyway."

"Good for your mom."

"Not only Mom. Jessie would put the hurt on any one of us who shirked his dishwashing duties."

Knowing his sister Jessie, Charlie laughed. "I love your mom and sister. They don't take any crap, do they?"

"No, and they're both killer poker players. It could give a man a complex."

"Or make him appreciate strong women," she said.

"True. I do like strong women," he said, with a pointed glance at her.

❧

DINNER AT HILDE'S Haus was always good. The old-fashioned diner wasn't fancy but it had good German and American food and it was a local favorite. Red-vinyl-covered booths occupied the edges of the big room, tables were scattered throughout the center and a counter ran half the length of the dining area. Paintings and wall art from local artists graced the walls, each with a discreet price attached to it.

Turner liked to experiment. He usually got whatever the special was, and if not that, he'd get the Wiener schnitzel. As she usually did, Charlie ordered the hamburger and fries. Another good thing about the diner was that they were speedy. No long dinners where you waited and waited for your server. Soon, Turner had the special, sausage and sauerkraut tonight, and Charlie her hamburger.

It occurred to him that he rarely heard her order anything else at the diner. "Why don't you ever get anything different here?"

"I get different things. Sometimes. But I really like the hamburgers. And their fries are wonderful." She eyed his plate. "I wouldn't say no to a bite of yours."

He laughed and offered her a bite. She ate it from his fork, closing her eyes and saying, "Mmm." Then she licked her lips and smiled at him.

Damn. The gesture went straight to his dick. He cast around for something to say to take his mind off what those beautiful lips would feel like on his body. "You've been awfully quiet since we left the shop. Is something going on?"

"Yes." She took another bite of her burger.

"Are you going to tell me what?"

She'd put down her hamburger and begun eating the fries. She pointed one at him and said, "We're dating. Exclusively."

Turner cocked his head. "Okay. So?"

"I still have reservations about you and me. About us dating. Officially. And you sneakily managed to make it happen anyway."

He knew it would piss her off but he couldn't help laughing. "You haven't voiced any complaints until now."

"That's because I didn't realize we were dating seriously until Josie pointed it out."

"What do you have against the two of us dating each other?"

"When I'm not mad at you—which, by the way, I am right now—I consider you one of my best friends. I don't want to risk that friendship."

"Neither do I. But why do we have to?"

"Because that's what always happens when you break up."

"Then we won't break up."

"You can't guarantee that."

"You can't guarantee that we will."

"You are the most infuriating man I've ever known."

It was difficult but he managed not to laugh. He put out his hand and said, "Give me your hand."

"Why?"

"Because I want to hold it." He barely stopped himself from adding, "Duh."

She grumbled but she wiped her fingers on her napkin and put her hand in his. "There, satisfied?"

"Not in the least, but it will do for now. What are you afraid of? What's holding you back?"

"I told you."

"We've hardly kissed and you already have us breaking

up. Why don't you give us a chance and see where it leads?"

Their waitress showed up and asked, "Can I get you two lovebirds anything else?"

Death rays shot from Charlie's eyes and she yanked her hand out of his. "We aren't lovebirds," she said, disgustedly.

"That's what it looked like to me."

"We're good, Sara," Turner said hastily, aware that Charlie was about to blow. "We'll take the check when you have a chance."

After dinner they walked back to the shop to pick up their cars. "Still mad at me?" Turner asked Charlie.

"Yes."

He studied her for a minute. She looked more annoyed than angry. "Does this mean you don't want to watch a movie together?"

"Brilliant deduction, Sherlock."

"It's one of your favorites."

"Ha!" She looked at him suspiciously. "What is it?"

"I'll give you a hint. What was the stuffed animal I gave you?"

"A dog."

"What kind of dog?"

"A Saint Bernard..." She stared at him. "You didn't."

He just grinned.

"You got *Beethoven*? The movie *Beethoven*? Really?"

He knew Charlie considered the old movie a classic. The story about the big, slobbery Saint Bernard was one she'd always loved, saying it made her laugh every time. "Yep. And it wasn't easy to find a DVD of it. I finally had to order it off the internet. We could have streamed it but I know you like DVDs."

"You fight dirty," Charlie said.

"I don't want to fight at all."

She still looked undecided.

"If it's that big of a deal you can watch it without me. It's in my car. I can go get it," he added.

"You might as well come over and watch it."

"Such enthusiasm."

"Do you want to come over or not?"

"I want to come over. But only if you want me to. I don't want to have to twist your arm."

"You're going to make me say it, aren't you?"

Figuring it was a rhetorical question, he simply lifted his shoulders.

She huffed out a sigh. "All right. Turner, would you please come over and bring the movie with you?"

"Why thank you, Charlie. I'd be happy to."

Chapter Six

TURNER NOT ONLY brought the movie with him, he brought triple chocolate ice cream. Damn it, he knew all her weaknesses. He was seducing her, not with expensive gifts but by giving her things that proved how well he knew her. Movies and books she loved, the shirts and mugs and other things with all the pie sayings, flowers, a huge stuffed animal... How was she supposed to resist all this? And then there were the kisses, making her imagine what going further would be like. As she spooned ice cream into two bowls, she pondered what to do.

She still had a lot of reservations. She knew Turner as well as he knew her. If they became lovers, he would want more. Eventually. And by more, she meant marriage. Turner would want what his parents had. A long, happy marriage. A family. Children. The one thing she couldn't give him.

Maybe she was wrong about what Turner wanted. Maybe he didn't want anything long-term and she was misreading the situation. After all, he'd never actually said. Shouldn't she give him a chance? Give the two of them a chance? Especially when that was what she wanted too?

She took the ice cream into the den and saw that Turner

had set up the DVD player. "I love this ice cream," she said, handing him his bowl.

He gave her a wicked grin. "That's the idea."

The movie was just as she remembered it. Cute and funny. It was a feel-good movie, one of her favorite types.

"I'd better get going," Turner said after it ended. "We both have work in the morning."

"Wait. I want to ask you something and I don't want you to blow me off."

"That sounds ominous."

"I'm serious, Turner."

"I can see that you are. What is it?"

"If we get together—" She hesitated, trying to frame her thoughts. "What if we get together and it doesn't work?"

"We already talked about that. Then we'll still be friends. We can do that. We just have to want to."

"What if it does work out? Where do we go then?"

"I never knew you were such a worrier."

"That's no answer."

He looked at her for a moment, with that half smile she found so appealing, and then he cupped her face in his hands and kissed her. It was both sweet and sexy. His mouth moved over hers with slow deliberation, teasing her, testing her, promising all manner of things. Sexy, exciting, and oh, God, so, so tempting.

She moved her hands, but only to put her arms around his neck. She was so tired of fighting this attraction. So damn tired of denying her feelings. So tired of looking at him and wanting to kiss him. And more. She pushed him back and kissed him again, and soon she lay on top of him, the full length of her body pressed up against his, and the kiss exploding into passion. His hands on her butt, holding her close, letting her feel him growing hard even through their jeans.

She felt his hand on her breast and wanted it on her bare skin. She pulled back and jerked her shirt off over her head. This was too much, too fast, but she didn't give a damn. He reached behind her and popped her bra open. Then slowly drew it off and flung it aside. And then she felt his hands cupping her breasts. She opened her eyes and watched him. He looked so serious.

"God, you're beautiful. I knew you would be."

She leaned down and kissed him again, exploring his mouth with her tongue, a slow tango of seduction.

His phone rang. They both stopped and stared at each other, Turner with his hands still on her breasts. He closed his eyes and groaned. "Damn it."

"Do you have to answer it?"

"It's the hospital. Their ringtone."

That answered that question.

He reached over to the coffee table and picked up his phone. Charlie managed to roll off him and stand up, then went searching for her shirt. Tugging it on over her head she heard him talking, asking for details. Vitals, she understood. Other things he talked about, not so much.

Finally, he ended the call. He sat up and shoved his hands through his hair. He looked up and met her eyes, regret in his gaze. "I have to go to the hospital."

"I kind of gathered that. I thought you were off tonight?"

"Technically I am. But this is one of my patients, so if I'm available, I take care of them." He shrugged and got up and so did she. "About tonight, I didn't mean to—"

She put her fingers on his lips. "Shh. I wanted that as much as you."

He grinned. "I doubt that."

She smiled in return. "Go to the hospital. We'll talk later."

He started to say something. Instead, he kissed her. She kissed him back. "Go," she said, pushing him toward the door.

She closed the door behind him, and pressed her back against it, palms flat against the door. Oh, God, how did that get so hot so fast? Probably because they'd been working toward it for weeks...months...years?

Was she ready for this? He hadn't answered her when she asked where they would go next. Except that he had, when he kissed her. And if he hadn't gotten that call they'd have been in her bed, making crazy love.

You're afraid. Afraid of what becoming lovers will do to your friendship...and you're afraid that if you do become lovers Turner will want more. And so will you.

TURNER FINISHED UP an operation on a man who'd fallen and fractured his skull and thanked God it had been a success. But it had been touch and go for a while there. He changed out of his scrubs and decided he needed pie. Really, he needed to see Charlie. He hadn't talked to her since he'd left her house the night before. He'd spent most of the night at the hospital with his patient and then today, he'd operated on the man with the skull fracture, which had taken most of the day. Since it was almost her closing time, he decided to see if he could talk her into having dinner with him. And talk about what had almost happened between them. Because he didn't doubt that had his phone not rung, he and Charlie would have made love.

He opened the door and the bell jangled, but neither Charlie nor the man who was talking to her appeared to notice. Rick Wallace, who was leaning on the counter and very obviously flirting with Charlie.

Typical. Damn it, why was it every time he saw Wallace lately, he was hitting on Charlie?

"Are you sure I can't convince you to change your mind?" he heard Rick say.

"Afraid not," Charlie said. "We've been through this before, Rick. I'm not going out with you again. Besides, you know you only keep asking me because it hurts your pride that I was the one who called it quits."

"Ordinarily you'd be right. But not this time. We were good together, Charlie. I care about you. Can't you give us another chance?"

She started to answer but then she caught sight of Turner. Her eyes lit up when she saw him. It made him feel good, except he was fairly sure that part of why she was glad to see him was because his presence would put an end to

Rick continuing to badger her for a date.

"Turner, hi! You're early," she said, her eyes begging him to play along with her.

Which he was totally happy to do. "I finished sooner than I'd thought I would, so I came on over. I hoped you might get Audrey to close up so we could take off early."

"I would but she wasn't feeling well and went home a while ago. But it's not too long until closing time now."

Rick, who'd been looking from one to the other of them, said, "Well, damn. I knew you'd gone out together but I didn't think anything of it. Why didn't you just tell me you and McBride were together, Charlie?"

"Yes, Charlie, why didn't you?" Turner asked, enjoying himself.

"Because it's none of your business," she said to Rick. "But now that you know, you can give it a rest."

"You're a cruel woman, Charlie. See you later, Turner. You'd better treat her right."

"No worries there."

"Thank you," Charlie said after Rick left.

"You're welcome." He waited a minute and asked, "Are we together now, Charlie? Because there's nothing I'd like more."

She got out a plastic bottle of glass cleaner and some paper towels and began to wipe down the display case. "If you hadn't gotten called away, we'd have made love last night."

"We were headed that way," he agreed. He watched as she came around front and carefully sprayed the glass and wiped it clean.

After a long moment, she looked up at him. "I don't know whether I'm frustrated because you had to leave or glad because I'm afraid it would be a mistake." She tossed the paper towels in a trash can, walked to the door and turned the sign around to Closed.

"I know which one I am. Frustrated. Definitely frustrated."

She chuckled. "Somehow, that doesn't surprise me."

"What can I say? I'm a guy."

"Turner, if we become lovers, everything will change between us."

"You think if we have sex we won't be friends any longer?"

"No. But I think once it's over, we won't be friends anymore."

Once it's over? They hadn't even slept together yet and she was already talking about the breakup. "Why does it have to be over?"

"Because nine times out of ten, that's what happens."

"Maybe we'll be the one time."

"But we can't know that."

He knew when to table a discussion. "I have an idea."

"What?"

"Let's go eat. You promised me a date, you know. It's the least you can do after I rescued you from Wallace."

She threw him a grateful look. "I suppose it is. I've been craving Mexican food. How about we go to Valencia's?"

"Great." Valencia's was one of his favorite places to eat. Nothing like a good Tex-Mex meal.

"Since we're going to dinner, I take it you don't want pie?"

"I always want pie. Maybe we can swing by after we eat?" he asked hopefully.

Charlie smiled. "You have an incurable sweet tooth."

"Don't expect me to argue about that."

Something dinged in the kitchen. "I've got to take some pies out of the oven," Charlie said.

He followed her back to the kitchen. "Where were your customers? You're usually busy right around closing, aren't you?"

"It depends. Most of the time. Obviously, not always. Kolaches is having an event," she said, speaking of the town's German bakery. "Free kolaches, a book reading and a book signing. I imagine most everyone was either already there, going there, or had been there and didn't need pie."

He leaned a hip against the counter and waited for her to finish. She picked up the pizza shovel, the long wooden paddle she used to take pies out of the oven or put them in, and opened the door to the industrial-sized oven. "I can leave these pies to cool," she said with her back to him, "but I'll have to come back by after dinner to put them in the fridge."

He didn't respond, being too busy looking at her ass. God bless women in tight blue jeans, he thought, watching her as she took out a pie. Usually Charlie wore her chef's apron when she was in the shop, but today she just wore jeans and a shirt.

Looking at her ass got him thinking about—what else— sex. But since she still hadn't decided about the two of them, he tried to put sex out of his mind.

Yeah, like that's working. Especially after last night.

"Last one," Charlie said, carrying the pie over to her cooling stand.

He was smiling, about to make a comment, when he saw her fall backward and go down. The pie she'd just taken from the oven flew off the shovel, which fell halfway on top of her with a loud clatter as the handle hit the floor.

"Charlie!" Turner ran over and fell to his knees beside her. She made a weird sound halfway between a groan and a cry and then nothing. She lay unmoving on her back on the hard brick floor. "Charlie, are you okay? Answer me."

But she didn't. He felt for her pulse, reassured when it beat steadily beneath his fingers. Her eyes were closed and she was unconscious, which did not reassure him at all. Blood seeped from beneath her head to spread in a pool across the kitchen floor.

My God, the blood. He was accustomed to blood, and lots of it, but usually he was in the operating room in a controlled atmosphere. Or he was bleeding from a minor cut. But he sure as hell wasn't used to seeing blood gush from Charlie's head.

He got up and grabbed a white cotton dish towel from a stack of clean ones on the counter. Gently, he raised her head and placed the folded towel beneath it, keeping his hand beneath her head to add to the pressure. Although he wanted to look, he knew the important thing right now was to put pressure on the wound.

Turner yanked his phone out of his pocket and dialed

911. The dispatcher answered, "Nine one one, what is your emergency?"

He put the phone on speaker and laid it down beside him. "This is Dr. Turner McBride. I have an unconscious woman with a concussion and possible skull fracture. I need an ambulance immediately. At Char-Pie on Main Street."

"How long has she been unconscious?"

"About two minutes. I started timing it right before I called you." Two minutes and counting. "Charlie, wake up."

Still no response.

"She's bleeding heavily and is still unconscious," he told the dispatcher.

"I'll dispatch the ambulance right away. Do you want me to stay on the line, Dr. McBride?"

"No, I've got it. Tell them we're in the kitchen."

He hung up and checked the time. Two minutes forty-six seconds. "Damn it, Charlie, wake up." He patted her cheek, willing her to wake.

Her eyelids fluttered. Slowly, her eyes opened. She stared at him as if she had no idea who he was.

"Do you know what happened?" he asked her, relieved she'd regained consciousness. But the fact that she'd been out for nearly three minutes was troubling. Very troubling.

"No. Where am—?" She started to get up and gave a cry of pain. "What—what happened?"

He put his free hand on her shoulder to keep her still. "Don't move. You fell and you have a concussion. You must have slipped on something." He looked around and spied a couple of what looked like cherry pits on the floor near where she went down.

"I fell? Why?" she asked hesitantly.

"I think you stepped on a cherry pit. No, lie still," he said when she attempted to get up again. "The ambulance is on its way."

"Ambulance?" she asked, sounding alarmed. "I don't understand. Why is an ambulance coming?"

"You fell and hit your head," he repeated. "You have a concussion."

"Oh. But I don't need an ambulance. I'm okay." She touched the back of her head, frowning when she ran into his hand holding the cloth. "What are you doing?"

"Keeping pressure on your cut."

"Cut?" She pulled her hand away and looked at it. "I'm bleeding. I don't remember...why am I bleeding?"

"Leave that alone," Turner said sharply, when she tried to move his hand. "You're not okay. You have a concussion, so do what I tell you and be still."

Subsiding, she closed her eyes. "My head hurts."

"A concussion will do that to you. Damn it, Charlie, you scared the hell out of me."

Chapter Seven

"HOW'S CHARLIE DOING?"

Turner looked up to see his brother Graham in the doorway of Charlie's ICU room. "Okay. So far." So far being the operative words. Waiting was hard with any patient but it was a killer when it was someone you cared about. He got up, both to stretch his legs and to talk to Graham without disturbing Charlie.

"I thought you said the CT came back negative," Graham said as they stepped out in the hallway. "That's what Spencer told me in his voice mail, anyway."

"I did, but you know as well as I do that even a negative CT doesn't guarantee she won't develop a brain bleed." He did *not* want to operate on Charlie, but if it came to that, he wouldn't trust anyone else to do it.

"Unlikely at this point, wouldn't you say?" While Graham was a cardiothoracic surgeon, he was also familiar with concussion protocol.

"Unlikely doesn't mean it can't happen," Turner said grimly.

"Spencer said you were a wreck when they got to the shop."

Their brother Spencer had been on call for EMS and had been one of the paramedics taking care of Charlie. They'd gotten lucky there, Turner thought. All the EMS teams were good but he trusted Spencer more than anyone else. "I was," he admitted. "God, Graham, she scared the hell out of me. I think I've aged ten years since she fell." He squeezed the bridge of his nose. "She was out for almost three minutes. And the blood—it was everywhere. Shit, what if she'd had a skull fracture?"

"She didn't." He studied his brother before saying, "You're doing what doctors always do when a loved one is hurt. You're thinking worst-case scenario. It's where your mind automatically goes."

Turner peeked in the room before he answered Graham. "Yours would, too. In fact you've probably already gone there."

"Maybe, but I'm not a neurosurgeon. You're programmed to think the worst in the case of an injury like this. But given what you've told me, there's no reason to believe Charlie won't be fine."

Turner shrugged, aware he wasn't being completely rational. But this was Charlie they were talking about. Being a doctor could be a blessing or a curse. He knew as well as Graham that doctors tended to overreact when someone they…cared about was injured.

"You look like hell," Graham told him. "And you've got blood all over you. Why didn't you change into scrubs?"

He looked down and realized Graham was right. "I was a hell of a lot more concerned with Charlie than I was with changing clothes."

"She's stable now. You should go home and get some rest."

"I'm not leaving her." He, of all people, knew what could happen with a grade three concussion. "She needs someone to take care of her. To keep an eye on her." There was a nice, comfortable reclining chair by the bed. He'd slept in worse before. Not that he planned to get a lot of sleep.

"She'll be fine. The nurses will take good care of her."

"I know they will, but they're busy. They can't drop everything to tend to one patient. I can." There was no way he was leaving her yet. It was his job to worry; to anticipate what could go wrong and do everything he could to make certain nothing did. "I'm staying."

"You realize you're totally in love with Charlie, don't you?"

"I'm not in love with her." Yet.

"Keep telling yourself that," Graham said. "It sure as hell didn't work for me."

"That's because any fool could see you and Bella were meant for each other." Graham and Bella had gotten engaged shortly before Charlie's accident. He was happy for them, especially since Graham had been so bummed that he was impossible to be around.

"Isn't she something?" Graham asked. "Bella has really changed my life. Everything seems all shiny and new."

Shiny and new? WTF? "Good God, Bro, you have it bad."

Graham grinned. "Can't deny it. But enough about me.

Want me to bring you something to eat?"

His stomach chose that moment to growl. "It's late. Nothing in town is open except for the convenience store. Thanks, but I'll just get something from the vending machine."

"Okay. Why don't you let me stay with her while you change and go get some food?"

He didn't want to leave her but if he was going to pull an all-nighter he needed something to eat, maybe a quick shower and definitely a change of clothes. "Okay, thanks." He started to leave but turned around and asked, "Why are you here so late? Are you on call?"

"No. But I had an emergency surgery five minutes before I was going to leave. It ran long. After hearing Spencer's voice mail about Charlie, I stopped by to check on her. And you."

"Oh, well, thanks. I won't be long."

"Take your time. I won't leave her. I am a doctor, you know."

Turner smiled. "I've heard that."

Graham put his hand on Turner's shoulder and squeezed. "She'll be fine, Turner."

"I know." He told himself to think positively but it was hard. Impossible, really. No one knew better than he did that a seemingly minor head injury could actually be something much worse. He couldn't stand to think of the worst-case scenario with Charlie. But the thought was there—always there. No matter how many times he went over the facts and statistics in his mind, he knew it didn't matter when bad things happened to someone you cared about.

Someone you loved.

WHY DOES MY head hurt so badly? Charlie opened her eyes and looked at a white ceiling. It didn't look familiar. *Where am I?* She turned her head, yelping at the pain. "Shit, that hurts."

"Try not to move around," a familiar voice said.

"Turner?"

"Yes, it's me." He swam into her line of sight.

She blinked, trying to bring him into focus.

He picked up her hand and squeezed it reassuringly. "I'm here. Do you remember what happened?"

"Kind of." She thought about that, though it was hard to do anything through the throbbing pain. "Not really."

"You fell in the kitchen at the shop and hit your head on the brick floor."

"Oh. No wonder it hurts. This isn't the shop. Is it?"

"No, you're at the hospital."

Hospital. She didn't like hospitals. She couldn't remember why, though. "I was in an ambulance. You were with me," she said, beginning to remember bits and pieces. "The siren made my head hurt."

"Yes, you told us that." Still holding her hand, he smiled a little. "Several times. Very forcefully, as in, 'Turn that damn thing off.' Any nausea?"

"No. Oh, God," she said, recalling bits of the ride. "I

barfed on you. Didn't I?"

He laughed. "It happens with a concussion sometimes. Don't worry about it. I've had worse happen. Besides, it mostly missed. How's your vision?"

"I see you fine. At first you were fuzzy but you're not anymore. You're so pretty," she said.

Turner frowned. "Now I'm really worried."

"Why?"

"You've never called me pretty before."

"I wonder why?" Brown hair, beautiful blue eyes, a classically handsome face. Something was nibbling at the edge of her consciousness. "I remember...last night. No, not last night. But I remember kissing you. And...I'm not sure what else happened. Did we have sex?"

He frowned. "No, and never mind that. Is your vision blurred? Are you seeing double or anything like that?"

"No. There's only one of you." A very pretty one of him. "I want to go home."

"You can't. You have a concussion and need to stay here for observation."

"I don't want to stay here. I want to go home," she insisted.

He looked very solemn and held on to her hand. "You need to listen to me, Charlie. You have a grade three concussion. That's serious."

"A concussion? Why do I have a concussion? What happened?" She had a feeling she was supposed to know the answer to that question, but she didn't. "My head hurts," she complained. "Can you make it stop?"

"We're trying. You've had medicine. Hopefully you'll feel better soon." He released her hand, took out a pen flashlight and peered into her eyes.

She tried to turn her head but it hurt too much. "Stop that. It hurts."

"I know. I'm sorry."

"I want to go home."

"You're not going anywhere until I'm sure you're okay. Your CT scan came back negative. You don't have a skull fracture, but you lost consciousness for almost three minutes and you needed stitches for the cut in your scalp. That means you need to stay here for observation."

Charlie stared at him. "Why do you look so concerned?"

"It's my job. I'm a doctor, remember? But you don't need to worry. You're going to be fine."

She closed her eyes. "Good." After a moment, she opened her eyes. She couldn't decipher his expression. "Will you stay with me?"

"Count on it. I'm not going anywhere."

She closed her eyes again. The next thing she knew, she heard someone calling her name.

"Charlie, wake up."

Slowly, she opened her eyes to look into the prettiest blue eyes she'd ever seen. *Turner? What's he doing here?* "Where am—oh, I remember now. I'm in the hospital."

"That's right," Turner said, shining that damn flashlight in her eyes.

That, she remembered. "Stop that. I don't like it. It makes my head hurt more."

"Sorry. But you'll have to get used to it. What's my name?"

"That's a dumb question."

He half-smiled. "Answer it anyway."

"Turner."

"Good. What's your name?"

She frowned. "Charlie."

He asked her several more idiotic questions, which she supposed she must have answered correctly because he shut up after telling her she could go back to sleep. Just before she faded out, she said, "I'm glad you're here."

"I wouldn't be anywhere else." He squeezed her hand and she drifted away.

CHARLIE WOKE UP slowly, wondering why she felt like a jackhammer was tap dancing on her skull. *Oh, yeah. I have a concussion.* She turned her head and saw Turner, asleep in the chair beside her bed. Had he been there all night? From the vague memories she had of him waking her up and asking her stupid questions, she thought he had.

He wore scrubs and his face was shadowed with stubble. Fragmented memories flooded her mind of…last night? No, it must have been the night before. She remembered kissing Turner. Remembered him kissing her back. And more. But she wasn't sure what had actually happened and what was her imagination. And while she was certain they'd kissed, she couldn't remember what else had gone on. Had she taken off her shirt? She closed her eyes and remembered the feeling of his hands on her breasts. Oh, yeah. That was definitely true. Then she remembered she'd asked him if they'd had sex and he'd said no. Still...

What the hell was she doing? Nothing had changed. She was still and forever unable to have children. But that was only a problem if Turner wanted to get married and have a family. Wanting more than a friends with benefits relationship was not the same thing as wanting to get married.

He opened his eyes and smiled at her. She smiled back, thinking it was too bad he was so pretty. And hot. Very hot.

Pretty.

"Did I tell you that you were pretty last night?"

His smile widened. "Yes. A number of times."

"I barfed on you too, didn't I?"

"Yep. We talked about it yesterday. Don't you remember?"

"Kind of. I was trying to forget it." That was humiliating.

"You have a concussion. I forgive you."

"Gee, thanks. Why are you here? You look like you slept here."

"I did." He got up and pulled out his flashlight pen.

She remembered that damn thing. "Oh, no, you're not shining that thing in my eyes again."

He ignored her, of course. When he finished checking her eyes he asked, "What's your name?"

"Matilda."

He gave her a dirty look. "Who's the president?"

"Scooby-Doo."

"Smart-ass. You're better, obviously. Does your head hurt?"

"Like the entire high school is line dancing on top of it."

"That will get better gradually. Are you having any visual problems?"

"No, but I need to go to the bathroom."

He got up and stood beside the bed, holding out a hand. "Let me help you. You were pretty unsteady last night."

Sitting up, she said, "Please tell me you didn't come in there with me."

He laughed. "No, I asked one of the nurses to help. I knew you'd be pissed if I helped you and I wasn't letting you go in there alone. Do you know how many accidents occur in bathrooms?"

"No. Enlighten me."

"Smart-ass," he said again. She stood up and swayed. Turner's arm came around her. "Steady there. Stand here a minute and get your bearings."

She was wearing a hospital gown and it occurred to her that her backside was hanging out. She tried to reach behind her to hold it closed.

"What are you doing?" he asked as she struggled with the gown.

"I'm trying to close this damn thing."

"Oh, for God's sake, Charlie. I'm a doctor. I've seen naked female asses before."

"You haven't seen mine. Have you?"

He stopped walking and glared at her. "When I see your

naked ass, you'd better believe it won't be in a hospital and you won't have a concussion." He began walking again.

"When?"

"When what?"

"You said *when* you see my naked ass."

He looked at her for a moment, then smiled. "I did, didn't I?"

"Freudian slip?" Though she was teasing, she did wonder what he'd say.

He pushed open the bathroom door and she walked in. She shut the door and stood there a minute. She could have sworn he muttered, "You can bet your sweet ass on that one, darlin'."

Too bad she felt like hell.

On second thought, maybe it was a good thing she felt like hell.

Chapter Eight

I T TOOK MUCH longer than she wanted, but finally she was discharged from the hospital. Turner had been with her almost the entire time. "You're really sweet to bring me home but I could have asked someone else," she told him after she got in his SUV.

After leaving the hospital, he glanced at her, then back at the road. "It's no problem."

"Don't you have work?" she persisted.

"No. I'm off for the next few days."

Once at her house, Turner came inside with her. She'd talked to Audrey that morning and her sister had said she was recovered from her virus and not to worry about the shop. Which was a good thing, since Charlie still couldn't focus very well.

"How long am I going to have a hard time focusing?"

"It varies. But you need to take it easy and give your brain time to heal."

"I know you said I couldn't go to work today but if I feel okay, can I go tomorrow?"

"No."

"But—"

"We talked about this at the hospital. You can't go to work for at least a week, probably longer."

"That seems ridiculously excessive."

She saw his jaw tighten and knew he was annoyed. "What is my profession, Charlie?"

"You're a doctor." *Duh.*

"And what's my specialty?"

"I know you're a neurosurgeon but—"

"There is no *but*. My job is to take care of people with injuries like yours. So listen to what I'm telling you."

"You didn't operate on me. I'm not really your patient."

He gave her an incredulous look. "You sure as hell are. Are you trying to piss me off?"

To her utter humiliation, her eyes filled with tears. "I'm s-s-s-sorry," she said, and the tears flowed.

"Oh, hell," he muttered, and pulled her into his embrace. "No, I'm sorry. Go ahead and cry. I know it's hard when you can't do what you're used to doing."

She sobbed against his shirt, clutching the material, unable to explain why she was crying, though she tried.

"Stop," he said, and kissed her on the forehead. "Come on. You need to lie down."

He led her toward her bedroom. "Go ahead," he said, giving her a slight push. "We'll talk after you've rested."

"You don't need to stay with me."

"Apparently, I do. You don't seem to understand that you've had a serious injury. You can't rush your recovery. If you do, it will just take that much longer for you to get better."

She wanted to argue more but she was tired, her head pounded, and she felt slightly nauseated. So she shut her bedroom door, changed into her pajamas and got ready for bed. Then she opened the bedroom door and announced, "I'm going to sleep. Let yourself out."

"I'm staying."

The look in his eye showed a determination that she knew well. She would not win this argument. Nevertheless she said, "I'm fine. I don't need a babysitter."

"Go to sleep, Charlie."

"You're very bossy."

"It's one of my charms."

She gave up, shut the door and crawled into bed. Tomorrow, she'd argue with him. Surely, she'd be back to normal by then.

CHARLIE WAS SEVEN days out from the accident and Turner was having a hell of a hard time keeping her corralled. He'd stayed at her place her first night home, dozing on her couch so he'd be sure to hear her and could check on her easily, over Charlie's objections that she'd be *just fine*. After that she kicked him out. He went, but that didn't stop him from checking on her several times a day and stopping by every evening to examine her briefly, bring her food or see if there was anything else she needed. He was on call some of those days but he was able to arrange it to be able to stop by her house at least once a day.

Was he being overprotective? Yes. Was he overreacting? Yes. But whenever he thought about backing off, he'd remember another story of someone who died after hitting their head in a fall.

Sure, her parents called to check on her but Charlie had refused to let them leave Midland, where they'd been living for several years. He didn't think either of them realized, any more than Charlie did, how serious her accident could have been. At least Audrey was here. He'd had a long discussion with her. Knowing he'd need help to keep Charlie from overdoing it, he enlisted her sister's aid. Audrey was the only other person who Charlie would be likely to listen to. Although Audrey was younger by a few years, he knew Charlie respected her sister and business partner.

On the seventh day after the accident, he took her to the hospital and did a repeat CT. There was no sign of bleeding or swelling, or anything else to be concerned about, which made him feel a lot better. But he still couldn't convince Charlie how important it was to rest after a concussion. Her headache had abated and since she was going stir crazy at home, he cleared her to return to work gradually. Which meant clearing her to drive as well, but she promised she'd only drive when strictly necessary. He suspected their ideas of what strictly necessary meant were wildly different.

He took her home after the test. Before he left, he reiterated what he'd said before ad nauseam. He knew she was sick of hearing it, but hell, he was sick of repeating it. "I mean it, Charlie. Don't try to do too much. Go in and spend a couple of hours at the shop, but don't bake, don't do paperwork, and don't do anything that takes too much effort or thought."

"What's the point of going in, then?" she asked flippantly. "I'll just stay here the rest of my life, slowly going insane."

He gritted his teeth. "Do you want to get well?"

"You know I do."

He told her some stories—again—about concussion patients who had overdone things, returning to work too early, and the setbacks they'd endured because of that. Purposely, he did not tell her about the people who had died. The less she knew about that, the better. "The more you can take it easy now, the quicker you'll heal in the long run."

"Are you sure you aren't being overly protective?"

She was driving him bat-shit crazy. "It would be a lot easier for me to let you do whatever you want. But your health is too important to screw with. So suck it up and quit bitching. If you follow directions, you'll be better soon."

"You don't have to get grumpy about it."

"Yes, I do. Promise me, Charlie."

She sighed. "All right. I promise I will try to follow directions."

He raised an eyebrow. "You'll try?"

"Fine, I promise. Cross my heart." She traced an X over her heart.

"Good."

He turned to go but Charlie laid a hand on his arm to stop him. "Turner, I know I've been a cranky pain in the ass—"

"Not at all," he interrupted in a voice heavy with irony.

"Just a touch difficult."

She laughed. "I really do appreciate what you've done for me. Taking care of me and putting up with me and all."

"No problem. But do me a favor and don't have any more accidents."

"I'll do my best." She rose on her tiptoes and tugged his head down to kiss him on the cheek. "Thank you."

"You're welcome." He wondered what she'd have done if he turned his head and kissed her on the mouth. Really kissed her. But there were a number of reasons he didn't, every one of them a good one.

She was still his patient. Not only that, but she was by no means well. Considering what had almost happened the last time he'd kissed her, he couldn't afford to tempt fate. Not when her health was at stake.

CHARLIE'S DOORBELL RANG at 6:08 p.m. She knew from the timing that it was Audrey. Her sister showed up every day after closing. Though they closed at four, there was always prep work to be done before leaving for the day. Turner came by daily, but he was a lot more erratic about when. She got up to answer the door. "Hi, and yes, I'm fine, thank you."

"You look pretty good," Audrey said upon entering. She sat on the couch, tossing her bag down beside her. "You'll be glad to know everything is going well at the shop."

"Good. Now tell me the truth." Charlie knew that having complete responsibility for the shop with only part-time workers to help her was extremely difficult. She'd done it by herself when Audrey couldn't be there for one reason or another. And she also knew that Audrey wouldn't admit to anything she thought might worry Charlie.

"I'm telling you the truth. Candace is working out really well," she said of one of their part-time helpers who'd been full-time since the accident. "You know, we should consider hiring her full-time permanently. I think the extra money we'd bring in would more than cover her salary and with another full-time staff member, we could do a lot more. And we might even be able to take a day off occasionally."

"We can think about it and talk about it more. We'll obviously need her for a while. Turner said I can go back to work tomorrow. But only part-time." Remembering his list of restrictions, she frowned.

"Hallelujah," Audrey said. "Turner told me this afternoon."

"He stopped by the shop? Oh, you mean to get pie." She laughed. "He has such a sweet tooth."

"He bought a piece of pie but what he really wanted to do was to lay down the law about you."

"What about me?" Lay down the law? That didn't seem at all like Turner but Audrey wouldn't make up something like that.

"He made me promise not to let you take on too much. You're only supposed to work very limited hours at first and he went on and on about how important it is that you rest and be careful and a bunch of other crap. I'm surprised he didn't give me a sheet of paper with instructions on it."

"He gave that to me," she said dryly. "And he read it to me, too, since he forbade me to either read or watch TV at first. But even if he hadn't, I'm perfectly capable of following my doctor's instructions without him going around and enlisting you to hover over me."

Audrey nodded and grinned. "Turner said he knows you and he thought I should know your limitations in case you pushed too hard."

"That man can be so infuriating."

"He obviously cares about you." She paused and shot Charlie a considering look. "And I don't mean only as a friend."

Charlie colored but tried to make light of it. "Of course he cares about me. We've been friends forever."

"Uh-huh. Not to mention you've been dating. I don't suppose things have progressed any further than you've told me, hmm?"

The night before her accident had been anything but platonic. If Turner hadn't gotten that call from the hospital, they'd have ended up in her bed. She all but fanned herself thinking about it. Which must have shown on her face.

"Charlie! What happened?"

"Nothing."

Audrey raised an eyebrow.

"Okay, something happened. But it was a mistake."

"You slept with him!"

"No, I didn't. But things got heated." She went on to tell Audrey—more or less—what had taken place the night before her accident. "But he got called in, thank God, so nothing really happened."

"I wouldn't call a mad, passionate make-out session nothing," Audrey said dryly.

"I shouldn't have done it. But now I can't stop thinking about it. When my head doesn't hurt, anyway."

"Who can blame you? Turner is a good guy, Charlie."

"I know he is. But what do I do if we become lovers and then he wants more? I'd have to tell him I can't have children."

Clearly frustrated, Audrey blew out a breath. "Charlie, you're acting as if that's a shameful secret and it's not. Lots of people can't have kids for one reason or another. I don't think this is a problem you should worry about yet. Maybe you two will decide you're not suited after all."

"You don't believe that and neither do I."

"Okay, you're right about that. I still think your hysterectomy isn't anything you need to discuss yet. Seriously, you don't know that he wants to marry you and have kids, do you? Much less have *kids of his own*," she said making air quotes. "Which is a stupid phrase since any child you parent is a kid of your own."

"We haven't discussed anything approaching marriage or children." When Turner had told her he wanted more, that didn't necessarily imply he meant for keeps. Maybe she was projecting what *she* really wanted on to him.

"I rest my case," Audrey said triumphantly. "Relax and let whatever happens happen."

She could do that. Especially since it was what she wanted to do, too.

Chapter Nine

A T JESSIE'S REQUEST, Turner went out to the ranch a few days after the neurologist okayed Charlie to go back to work. While he didn't think she was ready, he wasn't her doctor anymore and he knew the neurologist was good.

Jessie had recently gotten a new rescue horse and she'd asked him to come out to the ranch to see what he thought about the gelding. And to help her shovel horse shit, if he knew his little sister.

Jessie ran the McBride ranch now. Their mother still had a hand in it, of course, and she still ran the cattle operation, but Jessie was turning it more and more into a horse ranch. Cattle ranching was no longer the mainstay of their business. Rita McBride wanted more time off to spend with her retired husband. Since there were three doctors in the family, the patriarch of the McBrides was always referred to as Doc McBride, or to his chagrin, old Doc McBride. At any rate, Rita was totally on board with Jessie eventually taking over the entire ranching operation. And if she wanted to concentrate on horses only, that was her prerogative.

As a young girl, Jessie had fallen in love with mustangs. So much so that from the time she could walk and talk, her goal had been to raise horses, and mustangs specifically. As a teenager, Jessie had begun rescuing mustangs and later breeding them. His sister was a cowgirl, through and through. She was also very astute. You only had to play poker with her to realize that this cowgirl had a razor-sharp mind. Not to mention, a lot of luck.

Even though they weren't close friends, Jessie and Charlie had known each other a long time. Maybe Jessie would know why Charlie was so reluctant to take their relationship further.

"Hey, Turner. How's Charlie?"

"Better. Going stir crazy."

"I can imagine." She peered at him closely. "Are you still worried about her?"

He shrugged. "Yes. I'd feel a lot better if I thought she wouldn't overdo it."

"That's probably hard for her. She likes to be busy. Don't you need to lie around and do nothing with a concussion?"

"Yes. You need to give your brain time to heal. It's important."

"The accident really scared you, didn't it?"

"Only the hell out of me."

"But she's going to be okay, right?" Jessie asked anxiously.

"She should be." Unfortunately, he often dealt with the things that didn't go right. Which gave him a slanted view of injuries. "Where's the new horse? A gelding, didn't you say?" he asked, changing the subject.

Jessie led the way to the barn. "Yes, a gelding. He's awfully thin. I don't think he was abused, but he was neglected. He doesn't seem to have a problem with people. Or at least, the people he's been around so far. That's one reason I believe he wasn't abused."

His coat was dark brown, his mane black and he had a blaze of white from his ears to his muzzle. When he saw Jessie, he nickered and hung his head over the stall door. "Hello, pretty boy," Jessie crooned, stroking his nose.

The gelding was far too thin to be pretty yet, but Turner could tell that he would be once he got some meat on his bones. He patted the gelding's neck, pleased that the horse didn't shy away from him. Like his brothers, having grown up on a ranch and rodeoed in his youth, Turner had an affinity to horses. "What did you name him?"

"Blaze. Because of the white blaze on his nose."

"He looks like a Blaze. Toss me a brush and I'll help you groom him."

"I never turn down a volunteer." She gave him a brush and they each took a side and started to work. "What's up, Turner? And don't tell me it's nothing. Not only were you uncharacteristically quiet during poker a few weeks ago, but you look like something is on your mind. Or should I say someone?"

The McBride family played poker on the tenth of every month. Everyone was expected to attend—only work or illness was accepted as an excuse not to be there. Turner suspected Jessie and their mother wouldn't consider death a good excuse either. Luckily, that hadn't been an issue.

"I wasn't quiet. Graham was bent out of shape over Bella. Everyone spent the evening giving him advice."

Jessie laughed. "Something must have worked since they're engaged now. But back to you—what's the problem?"

"There's no problem."

"Liar. Let me guess. You want to get together with Charlie and she says no."

He looked up from brushing and stared at her. "That's not exactly—"

"And by get together, I mean have sex," Jessie continued. "Have you done it yet?" she asked conversationally.

He was certain he blushed. "Jesus, Jessie! No."

"No you haven't or no you don't want to?"

"Yes. No. We haven't. Good God, have some class."

Jessie let out a peal of laughter. "I do. I said have sex rather than one of the alternative phrases."

"I really don't want to discuss my sex life with my little sister."

"Lack of sex life, you mean."

Turner gave her a dirty look.

Jessie propped her hands on her hips. "Oh for heaven's sake, Turner. You're in your thirties. I'd worry about you if you weren't interested. And I'm not only a grown woman, I breed horses for a living. Don't expect me to be shy about sex."

"Clearly you're not." He ran his hands through his hair, making it stick up in spikes. "Charlie says she wants to remain friends. She's afraid if we—uh—"

"Do it?" Jessie asked.

Turner winced. "She's afraid if we take our relationship to the next level, we'll ruin what we have."

"That's a reasonable fear."

"It would be if that was all I wanted."

"Have you told her you're in love with her?"

First Graham, now Jessie. "Why does everyone think I'm in love with Charlie?"

"Because you are. Have you told her?"

So much for thinking he could keep any secrets. He shrugged. "No. I'm afraid she'd freak out. In fact, I'm sure she would. She's only recently conceded that we could date. And now with her accident—" He shrugged.

"What are you going to do?"

"I don't know. Keep seeing her and hope she gets past this fear of losing our friendship."

"Good luck. And I mean that, Turner. You deserve to be happy and so does she."

"Thanks. Tell me something, Jessie. How did you know I was in love with Charlie? I hadn't figured it out myself until she had her accident."

"Are you kidding? Turner, you've been in love with Charlie Stockton for years. Ask anyone in the family. It's about time you did something about it."

❧

"I'M GLAD TO see you, Charlie," Charlie's friend, Joey Douglas, said. "Are you back to work full-time?" Joey was one of the town librarians and a regular at Char-Pie but Charlie hadn't seen her since her accident.

"Thanks, Joey. I am. It feels like weeks since I've been up to speed. Oh, wait, it has been."

They both laughed at that. Charlie felt like her old self now. No headaches or dizziness and only a little mental fuzziness now and then. Not to mention, her neurologist, Dr. Price, had cleared her to return to work full-time a couple of days before.

Turner hadn't been pleased when she told him, but what could he say? He was the one who had insisted she needed a neurologist. He said she didn't need a neurosurgeon and besides, he didn't want her as a patient anymore. A little insulted, she'd asked him why and he'd simply smiled and said, "You'll find out soon enough." Then he'd winked at her.

Which had made her stomach do a delicious flip-flop. Until Turner had hinted she hadn't considered it, but what if the reason he didn't want her as a patient was because he didn't think he should treat someone he was interested in? *Someone he wants to sleep with, you mean.*

Turner wasn't the only one who was thinking about the next level. That thought was very, very tempting.

So why don't you go for it, you dummy?

"Charlie? Is there something you want to talk about?" Joey asked.

"Uh, no. Why?"

"Well, I asked for a piece of cherry pie and instead of cutting a piece, you're kind of staring into the ether with a goofy smile."

"I didn't," she said, aghast.

"Not terribly goofy," Joey assured her. "Just a little."

"Oh, hell. I was thinking about Turner."

Joey smiled. "I see."

"You don't seem surprised."

"I'm very observant," Joey said.

Meaning she was that obvious? "Let's go sit down. I'll take a piece of pie myself. Do you want coffee?"

A short while later, they both sat down with pie and coffee. There were a few customers in the store but Candace had come back from her break and would take care of any new people who walked in.

Joey took a bite of pie and sighed happily. "You make the best pies."

"Thanks." She took a bite of hers before she realized she'd chosen Turner's favorite. Lemon meringue. God, she had Turner on the brain.

She and Joey had been friends for a long while but they'd become closer lately. Maybe she should talk to Joey about her dilemma. She knew from experience Joey gave good advice. "I'm wrestling with a problem."

"A man problem? Or business?"

"A man."

"So it's about Turner."

"Yes, Turner. You know Turner and I have been friends for a long time."

"Sure. Everyone knows that."

"Turner wants to um, take our relationship to the next

level."

"What does that mean? He wants to hook up? Or be friends with benefits?"

"I asked him that and he said he wanted more. When he kisses me, I don't care if I'm doing the best thing for us or not. I just want him."

"How do I put this delicately?" Joey asked. She sipped her coffee then set down the cup. "Have you slept with him?"

Charlie laughed. "That's not particularly delicate."

Joey lifted her hands in a 'what can I say' gesture. "I tried."

"No, I haven't. But he wants to. And so do I."

Joey's brow furrowed. "Okay, let me get this straight. You know each other really well and clearly like each other or you wouldn't have been friends for so long. He wants to be intimate with you and ditto for you with him. I don't see the problem."

"I don't want to hurt him. There are things about me he doesn't know. If we get serious, I'll have to tell him. That's the last thing I want to do."

"Are you sure you aren't inventing problems that don't exist?"

"What do you mean?"

"If the two of you are in love with each other—"

"We're not!" Charlie almost shrieked. "Who said that?"

"I don't know who said it, but everyone in town thinks it." Joey patted her hand. "I didn't mean to upset you."

"I'm not in love with Turner. And he isn't in love with

me."

Joey studied her briefly. "Okay."

"You don't believe me."

"I think you believe it. Or you're trying to anyway," she added, "But if you're not in love with him, why are you agonizing over the situation?"

That was a very good question. "Crap. I'm in love with Turner."

※

NOT LONG AFTER Charlie returned to work full-time, Turner called her. "Hey, how are you?" he asked when she picked up.

"I'm good. No, I haven't had a headache in days and Dr. Price is very pleased with my progress. So don't start with the lecture."

"Would I do that?"

"Yes. 'Charlie, you're working too hard. Charlie, you have to be careful. Charlie, don't overdo it,'" she mimicked.

"Excuse me for being concerned." Whatever she thought, he wasn't overreacting by wanting her to slow down and take it easy.

"You're excused. Is that why you called?"

"No. I called to see if you want to come out to the ranch this Saturday for poker night." Most of the time, poker night at the McBrides was family only, but from time to time someone brought a friend. And now that they were engaged, Graham was bringing Bella.

Turner had never brought a woman to poker night before. In his family that was tantamount to a declaration of love. Even his last girlfriend, who he'd been with for over a year, hadn't made the cut. According to Jessie, the entire family thought he was in love with Charlie anyway, so he figured it didn't make much difference.

Besides, he *was* in love with her.

"Tomorrow? You're inviting me to one of the famous McBride poker nights?"

"I am. Rita's fixing chili and corn bread," he said, speaking of his mother. "So how about it?"

"That sounds like fun. I'd love to come. I'll bring a couple of pies."

"Great. They'll love that. I'll pick you up around five thirty." He knew she closed the shop early on Saturdays and was closed all day Sunday. It occurred to him he'd never asked her if she even played poker. "You know how to play, don't you?"

Charlie laughed. "I guess you'll find out."

Great. She was probably as cutthroat as his mother and sister. On the other hand, maybe she'd give those two a run for their money. That would be fun to see.

Chapter Ten

THE MCBRIDE POKER night was well known in Last Stand. This was Charlie's first time to be invited and it was quite the experience. Jessie McBride had the reputation of being a card shark with the luck of the devil and after playing a few hands with her, Charlie could see why. Luckily, she was good herself, having learned early on, when their dad had taught her and Audrey. But she was no match for Jessie, and her mother, Rita, was just as good. In fact, they both bordered on brilliant. Bella Benson, Graham's fiancée and owner of Bella's Salon, had said she was brand-new to the game. Charlie noticed everyone helped her from time to time.

Having grown up in Last Stand, Charlie knew the whole family. She was a few years younger than Turner, which put her in between Spencer and Turner in school. Doc McBride had been her family doctor until he retired a few years ago. It was hard to keep up, since there were at least three and sometimes four concurrent conversations taking place. Bella was talking to Jessie about horses. Turner and his father were discussing sports, Spencer and Graham were talking about medicine and Rita had just asked Charlie if she'd had any recurring headaches or other problems associated with her concussion. All these conversations were going on at the same time as the game. And no one—except her—seemed to have any trouble keeping up.

Charlie looked at Turner, wondering if he'd put his mother up to asking her about her health. "I'm asking for me, not Turner," Rita said. "I've had a couple of concussions myself and it took me months to get back to normal after one of them." She made a face. "Tommy says it's because I tried to do too much too soon, but when you run a business, you don't always have a choice, do you?"

"No, you don't. Luckily my sister Audrey was able to take over the shop while I was out of commission but I know it's a lot of work, so I was anxious to get back to help her as soon as I could. I'm doing well now. I'm not sure Turner believes me but my neurosurgeon is pleased."

Rita nodded sagely. "The problem with doctors is that they know too much about the things that can go wrong. Instead of accepting that things are going well, they tend to worry about stuff a layman probably knows nothing about." She glanced at her husband fondly. "Tommy tries to keep those worries to himself. He does a pretty good job of it, most of the time."

"Turner didn't keep much to himself about my concussion. He warned me of all sorts of dire consequences if I didn't do exactly what he said."

Rita laughed. "I can hear him now. They tend to be worse with people they care about," she added sympathetically.

When it was time to have pie, they took a break from the game and Bella and Turner offered to help Charlie serve. "So we have requests for five blueberry cobblers and three pecan, right?"

"Four pecan," Turner said.

"But that makes nine. There are only eight of us."

"Someone wants both kinds."

"Someone meaning you?" she asked, lifting an eyebrow.

"I helped Jessie with the horses this morning," he said virtuously. "I should get a reward."

She laughed and served up the pie. After Turner left the room with the first batch Bella said, "This is my first time at family poker night. I wasn't sure what to expect, especially since I'm a newbie poker player."

"You play very well."

"Beginner's luck. And a lot of coaching. But thanks."

Turner came back to pick up more pie and left again. "I'm surprised you haven't been to more poker nights," Charlie said.

"We only got engaged last month, after poker night, and Graham never would ask me before that. Rita and Jessie tried to get him to bring me but he wouldn't."

"Why not?" she asked, puzzled.

"Graham said asking a woman to poker night was almost as good as a marriage proposal in his family. And since he was busy trying to convince himself that he didn't want anything permanent with me, he wasn't about to ask me before."

What the hell? Charlie didn't know what to say. As good

as a marriage proposal? "Turner and I aren't—we aren't even—we're not that serious. Do they all feel that way?"

"Oh, Charlie, I'm sorry. I didn't mean to imply that you and Turner were…well, you know. Graham is just super sensitive because of his ex-wife and how his family thought he'd never get involved with anyone again."

They said no more but Charlie hadn't needed anything else to make her worry about her relationship with Turner…and what would happen if they took it further.

※

"ARE YOU UPSET about something?" Turner asked Charlie on their way back from the ranch.

"No. Why?"

"I don't know. Partway through the evening, you got really quiet. Like something had upset you."

She twisted her hair around her finger. Something she did when she was agitated. "Why did you ask me to family poker night?"

Puzzled, he said, "Because I thought you'd enjoy it?"

"Is that the only reason?"

What was she getting at? "I've told you, it's pretty much a command performance, unless I want my mother and sister to make my life hell. So I had to go and I wanted to see you. It was a no-brainer to ask you to go with me." He pulled into her driveway and turned off the truck. "Why?"

She didn't answer that directly. "Do you want to come in?"

"Yes." She got out and he followed her. She unlocked her back door and walked in, tossing her purse down on the kitchen counter and heading for her den.

She wore a sleeveless white button-down shirt and tight-fitting blue jeans. She was barefoot, having kicked off her shoes the moment she walked in the door, like she always did. She looked great. As she always did to him. Turner realized it had been a long time since he'd been able to look at Charlie and not want to kiss her. Make love to her. Not while she was in the hospital, though. Then, he'd been too damn worried to think about anything but what might have happened and still could. But she was well now and according to her neurologist, none the worse for wear.

She sat on the couch and Turner sat beside her, totally mystified about what was bothering her. "Bella said tonight was her first family poker night, too."

"Yeah, I guess it was. Last month he was still trying to convince her to give him another chance."

"She said Graham wouldn't ask her before because in his family that was as good as a proposal of marriage."

He laughed. Now he got it. "That's a slight exaggeration. For the record, I'm not proposing. I wanted to see you, I asked you, you said yes, and we went to poker. It's pretty simple."

She covered her eyes with her hand. "I feel really stupid now. But the way Bella talked about it made me wonder what you were thinking."

"Charlie, look at me."

"No. I'm too embarrassed."

"Don't be. Besides, Bella's right that I wouldn't take just anyone." She uncovered her eyes and stared at him. "To be honest, you're the first woman I've brought to poker."

"I'm not sure whether to be flattered or worried."

"Neither." He put his arm around her and pushed up her chin with the other hand. Then he kissed her, but briefly. "You know what I want, Charlie. I want to be with you. I want to make love with you." *I want you to let me love you.* But of course, he didn't say that.

She looked into his eyes, her own a deep dark green. "Oh, Turner, that's what I want, too." She wrapped her arms around his neck and laid her lips on his. Instant fire and smoldering heat. She groaned and pressed closer, opening her mouth and teasing him with her tongue. Turner gathered her closer, wrapped his arms around her waist and kissed her back.

The kiss changed. Became more active, more sensual, more carnal. He changed the angle, crushing his mouth to hers. Thrust his tongue inside and tangled with hers. He wanted to drink her in, devour her, lose himself in her.

"Take me to bed, Turner."

He stood, swung her up in his arms and headed for her bedroom.

✦

CHARLIE KNEW SHE might be making a mistake. But she wanted Turner, and he wanted her. And for once, she was going to let the future take care of itself.

Turner set her down beside her bed. He smiled at her, rubbed his thumb over her lips. He kissed her, briefly, then his hands went to the buttons on her shirt. He undid them slowly, parting the fabric inch by inch as he did so. He reached the last one and pushed her blouse off her shoulders. She wore a lacy nude bra. She heard him suck in his breath before he unsnapped and took off her bra quickly.

"What?" she asked him when he simply looked at her.

He traced his fingers over her breasts, smiling when the nipples beaded. "You're amazing."

The look in his eyes made her feel beautiful as much as his words did. "Turner? Take off your shirt."

He pulled his T-shirt off over his head and tossed it aside. Then he gathered her close, bare chest to bare chest and kissed her. He pushed her back onto the bed, lying down beside her. He stroked her breast, teased her nipple with his thumb and forefinger and then replaced his hand with his mouth. She put her hands in his hair to hold him there, shivering at the liquid pull and rasp of his tongue over her nipple. Soon she was writhing, wanting more.

"Wait," she told him. She unbuttoned and unzipped her jeans, wrestling her way out of them. Wearing only her panties, she climbed on top of him and rubbed herself against his denim-covered hard-on.

Turner groaned. She did it again, rotating her hips and leaning down to kiss him. He endured it for a little while longer, then flipped her on her back and paid her back by rubbing against her.

"You should take off your jeans," she said huskily.

"Gladly." He rolled off her, then stood beside the bed and shucked his jeans and boxers, pulling a condom out of his pocket and tossing it on the bedside table. A condom they didn't need, at least not for birth control purposes. But she wasn't going to think about that. Not now, with a beautiful, naked man standing beside the bed. He watched her, smiling that sexy smile that made her want to rip off her clothes, except there wasn't much left to rip off.

She wrapped her hand around his cock and started to take him in her mouth but he stopped her. "I'll go off like a rocket if you do that. And I want to savor this time."

So she let go and he lay down beside her again. He slipped a hand beneath her panties and slicked his fingers over her, sliding them in and out of her until she bucked and gave a strangled moan. All the while they kissed, his tongue mimicking the motions of his hand. He stripped off her panties and continued his sensual torment.

"I'm going to come," she said, as her muscles tightened around his fingers.

"Good. I want to watch you."

He kept up the delicious friction, then used his thumb to rub her clit while thrusting inside her with his fingers. And she shattered.

"Beautiful," he said, and kissed her. Dazed, she watched as he reached for the condom and rolled it down over his cock.

She opened her legs, gasping as he entered her with a driving thrust and began to stroke in and out. She wrapped her legs around his hips and hung on tight while he drove them both higher and higher. Pulling out then thrusting back inside her. Over and over. He kissed her, and said her name as he climaxed and she convulsed around him in an orgasm so intense, she nearly fainted. They lay there a long, long moment, breathing heavily. Turner rolled on his back, bringing her with him.

"So," he said, his voice a deep rumble as he gently stroked her back. "Regrets?"

Charlie rose on her elbows to look down at him and laughed. "Not even a little." And she kissed him.

Turner stayed the rest of the night. She nearly told him her secret after they used both his condoms and he was talking about going out to buy more. But she didn't want to ruin the night, and wasn't ready to talk about it anyway. So she merely said, "You don't need to get more. It's taken care of." Which it was, but not in the way he undoubtedly thought.

He looked at her a moment, then smiled and lay back down. "In that case," he said, took her in his arms, kissed her and made love to her again. Turner was a tireless and inventive lover. She'd had no idea what she was missing or she'd have succumbed much sooner to temptation.

"Do you have to work tomorrow?" she asked him, long after midnight. She lay with her head on his chest and his arm around her, his hand caressing her bare skin as they talked.

"No, thank God. I'd be pretty useless if I did."

"I don't have to work tomorrow either. I do need to go in but not for long and not until later."

"Good. Because now that I've finally got you where I've been wanting you for months, I have a number of fantasies to enact."

She rose up on her elbow and smiled at him. "Do tell."

"I'd rather show you." He pulled her head down and kissed her, long, slow and sexy.

"I'd like that," she murmured against his mouth, and succumbed to the pleasure.

Chapter Eleven

TUESDAY NIGHT CHARLIE met a bunch of her friends at the Saloon for a special girls' night out that Bella Benson had planned. Their usual girls' night out was 'First Wednesday,' which as the name stated, took place the first Wednesday of the month. They varied where they went first but the group always ended the night at the Saloon.

Slater Highwater's Last Stand Saloon was one of the town's original buildings. The Saloon had even been the site of the battle from which Last Stand took its name. There were still bullet holes in the walls from the Mexican army trying to crush the Texians—but not succeeding—during the Texas revolution. The bar was a cozy place with a jukebox and pool table for entertainment, and not a TV to be found. An anomaly in this age of sports bars with fifteen different TVs blaring, but one the townspeople loved. Tourists loved it too. They all wanted to see the bullet holes and hear the history, which Slater was happy to tell—but not every night.

Since it was Charlie's turn to close up shop, Audrey was already there by the time Charlie arrived. The girls had shoved two tables together in the middle of the room and if the half-full pitcher of margaritas on the table was any indication, they were having a good time.

When she called everyone, Bella said she had an announcement to make, so as many of them as could wrangle it showed up. Tonight Charlie counted nine, no ten, of them, including Bella and Jessie, who Charlie hadn't seen since poker night at the McBrides' the weekend before.

"Wow, looks like I've already missed something big," Charlie said, pulling out the empty chair between Jessie and Lily Jones. She poured herself a margarita and asked, "What happened? Do you know, Lily?" As a reporter for *The Defender*, Lily was usually up on what was happening.

"No, but I have a suspicion."

Bella tapped her spoon on her glass to get everyone's attention. "I know you're wondering why I asked you all here. I wanted to share my news with as many of my friends as I could." She drew in a breath and announced, "I'm getting married!" She raised her glass before drinking.

"That's great, sweetie," Delilah Corbyn, one of Bella's best friends, said. "But didn't we already know that?"

"Yes, but we finally picked a date."

There was a chorus of "congratulations." When the excitement died down Josie Vance asked, "When is it, Bella?"

"That's the thing. It's a week from Saturday," Bella said. Everyone began speaking at once.

After things quieted down, Sage, Slater's sister, said to Bella, "That isn't much time to put together a wedding. How did you find a venue that was free that day?"

Bella said, "It's going to be at St. Mark's Episcopal. You

know, where the McBrides all go? The church suddenly had an opening for a week from Saturday. It seemed like a sign, especially when Delilah said we could change the date at her restaurant for the reception too."

Delilah Corbyn owned Dragonfly, a beautiful restaurant on the river. Since Delilah was one of Bella's best friends, it was no surprise she'd offered the restaurant for the reception.

Jessie added, "What she hasn't told you is my brother announced he was tired of waiting and if 'the women' didn't choose a date soon, he and Bella were eloping. 'The women' meaning Bella, me, and my mother. So when an earlier opening came up, we all jumped on it."

"I can see Graham saying that," Charlie said to Jessie with a smile. "I bet he'd follow through, too." Charlie had known Graham almost as long as Turner, but he'd been ahead of her in school so she hadn't interacted with him much.

"Oh, he would," Jessie said with a laugh.

"This calls for a toast," Emma Corbyn, Last Stand's head librarian said. Emma was shy and quiet a lot of the time, but she relaxed some when she was with her girlfriends. "To Bella and Graham!" Everyone raised their glass and toasted.

Shortly after that, a waitress brought over a couple of bottles of champagne—really good champagne—for the table.

"We didn't order champagne," Bella said.

"The boss says it's on the house."

They all looked at Slater behind the bar and waved thank you. Charlie suspected Joey had told him what was going on since she'd been at the bar talking to him not long before that. Either that or maybe he'd overheard the toasts. That wouldn't have been hard. The waitress passed out champagne glasses, the bubbly was poured and the happy couple toasted.

"Is it possible to be deliriously happy and nervous as hell at the same time?" Bella asked the table in general.

Sage Highwater answered, "Yes. Definitely yes. After all, you don't get married every day. And after hearing about Graham's proposal, I'm thinking he must be a true romantic."

"Oh, he is," Bella said in a dreamy voice.

Graham had proposed to Bella at her salon in front of half the town. From what Charlie had heard, it had been breathtakingly romantic. She hoped they'd be very happy. When she was at poker night, she'd thought Bella and Graham were obviously crazy about each other and even though they seemed very different, they also seemed to complement each other.

She didn't think every marriage was a failure. Obviously some worked out well. Who knew, hers might have worked out if she hadn't—

She cut off that line of thought. *Good God, what's the matter with me? Thinking about my failed marriage when I'm truly happy for Bella and Graham.*

"I'm going to need help deciding how to wear my hair," Bella said.

This should be interesting, Charlie thought. Bella, who was a hair stylist and owner of her own salon, liked nothing better than trying new hairstyles and colors. "You'll have to have us to the shop to try different looks."

"Maybe I should wear it rainbow-colored. That's what it looked like the first time we talked to each other."

Bella was one of those women who could wear any hairstyle, any color and look good.

"Do you have a dress?" Joey asked her.

"Now you've done it," Jessie muttered. "She cries—in a good way—every time she talks about it."

"Rita, Graham's mother, knew I didn't have a dress. She offered to let me wear her wedding dress. She said—" Bella sniffled "—Rita said she hoped I'd wear the dress as a token of my new family's love and my something borrowed."

"Don't forget old," Jessie interjected.

"I'm not the one who added that, thank God," Bella said, diverted from crying by laughing at that remark. "You and Graham are in deep trouble."

Jessie got up to hug her soon-to-be sister-in-law and everyone started talking again.

"A little birdie told me you and Turner are dating now," Sage said across the chair vacated by Jessie.

"Jessie, I take it."

Sage smiled. She and Jessie were good friends. The two families' ranches adjoined so they'd all known each other forever. "You got it. Is it weird dating a friend?"

"At first it was," she answered frankly. "Sometimes it still is. We've only recently started actually dating. Turner and I aren't serious," she said as Jessie returned. At least, she hoped he didn't think they were.

Jessie and Sage exchanged a glance that indicated they didn't believe her. "It's true. Just because we're having sex doesn't mean we're looking at anything long-term." Belatedly realizing who she was talking to, Charlie flushed. "Damn."

Jessie and Sage both burst out laughing. "Sage and I both breed horses, Charlie," Jessie said when she'd recovered. "I seriously doubt you can shock either of us by talking about sex."

"Maybe not, but I can shock *me*."

"Because I'm Turner's sister?"

"Well, yeah."

"Don't worry about it. I'm just glad to see the two of you finally getting together."

Charlie started to ask her what she meant by *finally* but someone else caught Jessie's attention and the moment was lost. But it did give Charlie a lot of food for thought.

TURNER FINISHED A long operation and was contemplating whether he should scrounge up something to eat or if he was too tired and should just go to sleep in the on-call room. His phone rang and seeing that it was Charlie, he answered it. "Hi. What's up?" She knew he was working tonight so he was a little surprised to hear from her. She didn't usually call him then.

"Can you go to the doctors' lounge?"

"Why?"

"You'll find out," she said and hung up.

Charlie was waiting for him in the lounge. "How did you get in here?" he asked after kissing her hello.

"Bribery." She motioned to a crowd of people surrounding one of the tables. He could see—barely—several partially eaten pies.

"Good plan."

"I brought you some dinner and some pie."

"That's really sweet but why?"

"Because I know you don't usually get to eat when you have a long day operating." She handed him a sack from Hilde's Haus.

He opened the sack and looked I inside. "Schnitzel. Looks great. Thanks." His stomach growled and Charlie laughed.

"Your stomach agrees."

"Do you think there will be any pie left?"

"I brought you your very own." She handed him the sack in her other hand.

"You are the woman of my dreams." He took his food to one of the empty tables and began eating. By the time he finished dinner and started on his pie, the room had cleared of people and all the other pies were gone.

"I saw Jessie last night at the Saloon. Bella told us she and Graham picked a date for their wedding."

"Graham told me this morning. I was working during the pow-wow." Something was going on with her but he couldn't tell what. Charlie twisted her hair around her finger but she stopped when she realized he had noticed. The hair twist was a sure sign she was conflicted about something.

"I think Jessie has the wrong impression about us."

"Why is that?"

"She said something about being glad the two of us *finally* got together. Like she thinks we've been heading that way for a long time. Or maybe she thinks the two of us are serious."

"We aren't?" Problem was, she might not be serious but he for damn sure was. And the last few nights with her, making love to her, had only clarified his own feelings.

"No, we're not. We've only just started—I mean, it was only last weekend that we—"

She broke off so he finished for her. "Became lovers? Had sex? Hit the sheets?"

"You're not funny," she said, flashing him a dirty look. "I told her we weren't, but I'm not sure she believed me."

He wanted to ask her why she was so sure the two of them weren't serious—that *he* wasn't serious anyway. But it was crystal clear she wasn't ready for that conversation. "Don't worry about Jessie," he said, making a mental note to talk to his sister about keeping her mouth shut. "She's trying her hand at matchmaking. I think she's taking lessons from Clara Perkins." Clara, the woman he and his brothers had nicknamed *The Matchmaker* and who had introduced Graham to Bella…who were now engaged and soon to be married. Clara's status among her friends had shot up into the stratosphere with that accomplishment.

"Why does it bother you?" Turner asked, setting down his fork on his now empty plate.

"Why does what bother me?"

"Why does it matter what other people think about something that's no one's business but ours?"

"It doesn't, really. But Jessie's your sister and I don't want your family to get the wrong idea about us. You already did that by asking me to poker night. And don't deny it."

He shrugged as if it didn't matter but Charlie's reluctance was beginning to grate on his nerves. "Since poker night was the night you and I first made love, don't expect me to regret asking you." He sure as hell didn't regret that night or any of the nights following it. They'd spent the weekend together and every night since until the night before. "I thought you said you had no regrets. Have you changed your mind?"

"No."

"Good." He didn't push for more. Instead he cupped her face in his hands and kissed her. "I'll see you tomorrow after work. Thanks for the food."

"You're welcome."

They both stood. "I'll walk you out," Turner said.

"You don't need to. You look tired. Go get some rest."

"I will, after I walk you out."

At her car he kissed her again and watched as she drove off. He reminded himself to be happy that they were together for now. He'd worry about the future later.

His phone rang and he went back to work. So much for sleep. At least he'd had some food.

Chapter Twelve

S INCE HE WASN'T working, Turner drove out to the ranch again the next morning. Jessie was out in the round pen, putting Blaze, the new horse, through what she called her "getting to know each other" routine. He climbed the fence to sit on the top rail and watch.

He could swear the horse already looked better. No surprise, since Jessie had a special plan for the horses who came to her underweight. There was no doubt his sister had a way with them. They loved her and clearly sensed that she loved them. Even the most recalcitrant horse eventually gave in to Jessie's brand of love and training. In jeans and boots, with her long brown hair pulled back in a braid and a battered cowboy hat on her head, Jessie was the quintessential cowgirl. He wondered if and when she would decide to settle down with a man. But although she dated, she often said her horses were a hell of a lot more dependable than the men she went out with.

Jessie finished up, then let one of the hands take Blaze to cool him down before grooming him. She walked over and climbed up nimbly to sit beside him. "What's up, Turner?"

Never one to beat around the bush, Turner said, "I want

to talk to you about Charlie."

"I wondered how long it would take you to do that."

Not very long. "Charlie is almost as skittish as one of your new rescues."

Jessie laughed. "She might not appreciate being compared to a horse."

"I'm not talking to her. I'm talking to you, and you know exactly what I mean. I don't think Charlie has a clue I'm in love with her. If she did, she'd probably break it off right now."

"Why? It's obvious she cares about you."

"Let's just say she's wary. She seems determined to believe that we'll break up and then won't be friends anymore." Turner shook his head. "She's so convinced of that, she had us breaking up before we even got together."

"That seems weird. Do you know why?"

"Not really. But I feel like there's something she's not telling me. Something in her past."

"Bella told me about what she said to Charlie on poker night. And that Charlie looked panicked."

"Yeah, that's a good description. And then when you talked to her Thursday night, that got to her too."

"All I said was I was glad you two had gotten together. I swear I meant nothing by that."

"I know. I'm not blaming you."

"I like Charlie. I think you're good together. I wouldn't do anything to screw that up. Purposely, anyway."

"I know," he repeated, because he did. He knew the answer before he asked but he asked Jessie anyway. "Has she ever talked to you about her marriage or her ex?"

"No, but that's not surprising. I don't think anyone around here knows what happened in California. Well, I'm sure Audrey does. Those two are close." She pushed her hat back on her head and looked at him sympathetically. "She's never said anything to you?"

He shrugged. "Random comments here and there. But—" He hesitated. "I think it's the ex but I'm not sure what he did."

"Did he abuse her? That would give her a reason for being so skittish about you two."

"I don't think so. She's never even hinted that was a problem. The only concrete thing I remember her saying was he was a bastard and she'd been a fool to think she could depend on him."

"She couldn't depend on him? Well, that's sure not the problem with you. You're Doctor Dependable."

He looked at his sister, trying to figure out that comment. "I can't decide if that's a compliment or an insult."

"It's a compliment, dummy," she said, lightly punching him in the arm. "You haven't been together all that long. Maybe she's not ready to think about the long term."

"Hell, it wasn't until last weekend that we—" He broke off and finished, "It's not as if I've asked her to marry me."

"But you would if you thought it wouldn't freak her out, wouldn't you?" his sister asked shrewdly.

"I don't know." That was something he wasn't ready to admit to Jessie, or even to himself. "But I do know I'd like to be with her without having to worry that she's going to take something I say wrong and bolt."

"Is there anything I can do?"

He shook his head. "I don't think so. But for God's sake, don't tell her I'm in love with her."

"Don't worry, I wouldn't. What are you going to do, Turner?"

"What can I do except give her time? And let her know she can talk to me."

"And love her."

"Yeah. That too." His life would be a lot easier if he didn't.

CHARLIE WAS CLEANING up and preparing for the following day when Turner knocked on the front door of the shop. She let him in, locking the door behind him. "Hi."

"Hi." He drew her close and gave her a long, heated kiss.

Laughing, she drew away. "I've still got a lot of work to do. If you're going to try to distract me, you'll have to go away."

"How about I help?" He began to bus the tables. "Where are Audrey and Candace? Didn't you say you'd hired Candace full-time?"

"I did. Candace had an appointment and Audrey had a date so they both left early. And you do not need to bus tables."

"I do if you're going to get out of here anytime soon. Don't you have a teenager to do this?"

"Normally, yes. But he's home sick and there wasn't time to get anyone else. Stop doing that. I'll get to it."

He dumped the dishes in the plastic bus tub and picked it up. "Relax. I do this every time I go to the ranch. Every time I eat there, anyway." He carried the tub to the kitchen and she followed.

"Well, if you insist, you can put those in the dishwasher and I can finish cleaning the kitchen. I'll do prep work tomorrow."

They worked quietly for a bit and then Turner said, "Graham asked Spencer and me to stand up with him. He said he couldn't decide, so he wanted both of us to do it. Bella's having Delilah, Joey and Jessie. The ceremony is going to be at the Episcopal Church and it's going to be just family and a few close friends. They've asked a ton of people to the reception. It's at Dragonfly," he said, speaking of Delilah Corbyn's restaurant by the river.

Charlie wondered what he was getting at. She didn't have to wait long to find out.

"The ceremony is at six and then we'll go to the reception after that."

"Okay. Do you want me to meet you at Dragonfly then?"

He stopped loading the dishwasher to look at her. "No, I want you to go to the ceremony with me and then to the reception."

"Isn't the wedding ceremony only for family and a few close friends? I'm neither."

"You're dating me. That counts. Besides, you've known

my family forever."

It was probably a bad idea for her to go to another wedding. Especially this one. A romantic wedding of two people who were madly in love with each other. His brother. She didn't want to daydream about what it would be like to marry Turner when she knew that was all but impossible. But Turner would be hurt and never understand if she didn't go with him. "Okay. Thanks."

He looked surprised. "I was prepared for you to argue with me."

"Me, argue?"

"Yes, you," he said and walked over to her. He took her in his arms and kissed her. Sighing, she put her arms around his neck and returned the kiss.

It grew heated immediately. She wore a multi-colored, sleeveless summer dress, loose and breezy, and his hands slipped beneath it to caress her butt. She moaned when his lips left hers to trail down her neck to her cleavage. Charlie yanked his T-shirt out of his jeans and pushed it up as far as she could. He let go of her long enough to rip it off. Wrapping his arms around her again, he kneaded her butt, slipped a hand beneath her panties and caressed her where she was hot, slick and aching.

"Wait," she managed to say. "We can't do this here." She shoved him away and took his hand. "My office has a nice, big, comfy chair."

"I think I can wait that long."

Once in her office, she locked the door, then had Turner sit in the chair and she straddled his lap and kissed him.

Long, slow, open-mouthed kisses that soon had both of them on fire. Slowly, she raised the hem of her dress and he helped her pull it off over her head.

Turner buried his head in her cleavage, undoing her bra at the same time. She gasped as his clever hands and fingers reached beneath the loosened bra to caress her breasts. He pulled the straps down her arms and she flung it away. She leaned back, reveling at the sensation of his mouth on her breasts, slowly licking and sucking her nipples until they stood at attention.

"Wait," she said.

"Wait? Are you kidding?"

"No, I want to take off my jeans."

She climbed off him and watched him smile when she pushed her jeans and then her panties down her legs and stepped out of them. "If you're okay with that." She sincerely hoped he was since she stood naked in front of him now and the way he looked at her set fire to her blood.

"Better than okay." He'd taken off his shoes and socks while watching her. Now he stood and stripped off the rest of his clothes. She made him sit and climbed on his lap once again.

Reaching down, she stroked him, feeling him hot and hard and growing harder and longer with the movement of her hands. He kissed her, steamy, carnal kisses while she positioned herself over him and impaled herself on his cock. They both groaned. "You're killing me," he gasped.

"It's...mutual," she managed to say.

She tightened around him and let him guide her with his

hands on her hips. Rocking slowly at first, then faster, reveling in the sensation of fullness and spiraling higher. Then she felt his fingers where their bodies joined and gasped as he shot her over the top, at the same time driving upward with a guttural groan. She felt him pulse, endlessly, as her orgasm spun out, shock waves rippling through her body until she collapsed against him.

He tugged on her hair until she lifted her head. Then he kissed her and said, "Wow."

Charlie laughed. Wow, indeed. "I'll never be able to look at this office the same again."

"Me neither," he said, and kissed her again.

CHARLIE SPENT THE next ten days working and spending every spare minute with Turner. She was happy. Happier than she'd been in a long, long time. Every once in a while, doubt crept in and she'd be reminded that nothing lasts forever. Especially not when there were secrets being kept. But then Turner would make her laugh, or kiss her, or simply hold her close and the doubts receded. For the moment.

The morning of Graham and Bella's wedding, Turner came by the shop as he often did when he had a few minutes. He'd worked the night before so she hadn't seen him. He kissed her hello and said, "Are you sure you don't mind driving to the ceremony? We can drop your car off afterward. Or you could come with Sage."

"Audrey's going to drop me off. She'll have plenty of time before the reception."

Julie Shaw, one of Charlie's long-time customers, entered just then along with her three-year-old son.

"Hi, Julie. What can I get you?"

Julie greeted both Charlie and Turner and said, "I need a pie to take home. Pecan, if you have it."

Turner had squatted down to talk to the little boy. He wore a checkered shirt, blue jeans, boots and a cowboy hat. "Hi, Roy. What's that in your hand?"

"Horse. My horse," the child said clutching it to his chest.

"Oh, are you a cowboy? Like your dad?"

"Yup. Like Daddy." He struck a pose, one tiny thumb hooked through his belt loop and the other hand still clutching the horse.

Turner looked up at Julie, laughing. "He looks more like Ed every time I see him. Down to the boots and hat."

Julie smiled. "Yes, he's the spitting image of his father, isn't he?"

"I'll say."

As she boxed up the pie, Charlie smothered a pang. *The spitting image of his father. Oh, get over it,* she lectured herself. *You can't be so sensitive.*

"Kid's a pistol," Turner said after they left. "It's funny how some kids look exactly like their parents and others, nothing like them. Well, not funny. It's genetics, but you know what I mean."

Charlie made a non-committal sound and pretended to

clean off the counter, hoping Turner would quit talking. But of course, he didn't.

"The family has a pool going on how soon Graham and Bella will have a kid. I told Graham he better pray the kid looks like Bella."

"Why? It's not like Graham is ugly."

"I know but I like to give him shit. He's claiming they won't have one for a while but I don't believe it."

Here's your perfect opportunity. "You've never said if you want kids."

He looked a little surprised. "Sure. Someday. Not anytime soon—" He broke off and stared at her. "Are you pregnant, Charlie?"

"No. I was just curious what you thought about the subject."

"You'd tell me if you were, wouldn't you?"

"Of course. I'd never keep that from you." Not that there was any possibility of that happening. She turned away, aware she was about to cry and totally lose it. "I've got to take a pie out of the oven."

Turner was still there when she returned. She'd known he wouldn't leave without telling her goodbye. She pasted on a fake smile and hoped he wouldn't notice.

"Are you okay?"

"Yes, I'm fine."

"You seem upset. What's wrong?"

"Nothing. I have a headache and I can't leave until noon. We close early today for the wedding."

He didn't look like he believed her but at least he pretended he did. "Okay. I'll see you tonight." He took her hand, tugged her forward, leaned over the counter and kissed her. "Take care of that headache."

At least she'd have several hours to try to get the image of Turner with that little boy out of her mind.

Chapter Thirteen

G RAHAM McBRIDE'S AND Bella Benson's wedding ceremony was held at St. Mark's Episcopal Church on Wisteria Lane, where the McBrides had been members for decades. It was a beautiful old church with polished dark wood pews, stained glass windows, and red carpeting. A carving of Jesus on the cross hung over the altar and several carvings of saints were placed throughout the sanctuary.

Just as Turner had told her, only family and close friends of the couple were invited to the ceremony. The Highwaters, long-time neighbors of the McBrides, were all there, along with the Corbyns and a few others she didn't know. Sage Highwater sat next to Charlie. She'd known Sage a long time, although Sage was a lot closer to Jessie's age than hers.

"You look beautiful, Sage." Her dress was a bluebonnet blue, the same color as her eyes. Sleeveless, with a fitted top and accordion skirt, the style suited her perfectly. Since Sage almost always wore jeans, it was interesting to see her in a dress.

Sage laughed. "I clean up okay. Speaking of looking beautiful, so do you. Turner couldn't take his eyes off of you when you got here."

"You're sweet, but you exaggerate." Charlie wore a navy sleeveless chiffon dress with a high neck and asymmetric hem. She knew she looked good, but hardly beautiful.

"About you looking beautiful or about Turner?" Sage shook her head. "If anything I didn't go far enough about him. He's really stuck on you. You can tell just by the way he looks at you."

The service started a short time later. When Graham, his brothers and his father were all standing waiting for the bridesmaids and bride, Sage leaned over and whispered, "Those McBride men are enough to make me think tuxes should be required more often."

"I agree," Charlie said with a laugh. "They are a good-looking bunch." In her mind, of course, Turner was the most handsome of them all.

Jessie, Delilah and Joey all wore black short dresses, though each one was different. Smart, Charlie thought, to have them wear something they probably already had and could wear to other functions. Then Bella came in, walking by herself down the aisle, to a gorgeous classical piece of music Charlie didn't recognize. Graham looked as happy as she'd ever seen him.

Charlie couldn't blame him for not being able to drag his eyes away from Bella. She wore her blond hair natural, which was unusual in itself, gathered in a bun of loose curls at the nape of her neck with intricate braids on either side of her head. Her dress—Graham's mother's, she remembered—was a lace and chiffon wedding gown with capped sleeves, a scoop neckline, and a pearl beaded fitted bodice that gradually flared from hips to hem. Lace circled the hem of the dress and it had a long, lacy train. Everything about it was beautiful and elegant and perfect for Bella.

Oh, God, don't let this be an even bigger mistake than the last wedding I went to with Turner. At least then, she hadn't been dangerously close to falling totally in love with him. Or maybe she had been and had refused to admit it. But now she wondered about herself and Turner and whether they could—*No. No, no, no. Do not even go there.*

Turner was standing up for his brother, so at least he wasn't at her side, holding her hand. But every time she looked at him, she found him already looking at her. And the glances he sent her weren't heated. No, they were worse—they were loving. As if he imagined her up there, standing beside him.

But that was foolish. Turner hadn't said he loved her, hadn't pushed for more than they had. She was projecting, giving him thoughts and feelings that she had herself. Thoughts of forever had probably never entered his mind.

And what if they do? Now that you know for a fact he wants kids.

I'm not doing this, she told herself as she pushed the thoughts out of her mind. She meant to enjoy the beautiful wedding.

The Episcopal priest in his robes began the service. Graham and Bella said their vows—not ones they wrote themselves but the traditional ones, which surprised Charlie, given that Bella was very much a free spirit. But then, Bella often did the unexpected. The priest said, "You may now kiss the bride," and they kissed to the applause of the guests. Charlie had a lump in her throat the size of a baseball. They truly were a beautiful couple and were so obviously happy.

After the wedding party walked back down the aisle, the whole group congregated at the back of the church to congratulate the bride and groom before the reception, which Charlie suspected would be a bit of a madhouse.

"Well, that was almost worth wearing a tux for," Turner said as they walked to his car.

Charlie laughed. "It was a beautiful ceremony."

"Yeah, it was nice." At the car, he stopped and kissed her before opening her door. "You look gorgeous."

"Thank you, but you already told me that when I first saw you tonight."

"Worth saying again. Looks like everyone is headed out to Dragonfly."

"It's going to be a blowout, isn't it?"

"Absolutely," Turner said.

"And you're going to dance with me, right?"

"Every dance if you want."

"You'll be sorry if I take you up on that."

"Believe me, Charlie. Dancing with you is no hardship."

"DELILAH, HOW DID you manage all this when you were at the wedding until just a little while ago?" Charlie looked around Dragonfly at what she could only call a fairyland. Tiny white lights were hanging from the ceiling and strung around beams in the main room. Banks of large sparkling glass windows ran along the walls that faced the river.

Scattered throughout the main dining room, gorgeous flower arrangements graced white tablecloths on round tables. Mason jars with baby's breath were hung on the back of each white wooden chair. The dark wood floor was buffed and polished to a beautiful gleam and a space was cleared to make room for a dance floor.

The party spilled out down the rock steps onto the bricked terrace, which overlooked Hickory Creek. Round tables and white chairs held the same decorations as those inside. More tiny white lights were strung all around and a number of the trees and bushes nearby were lighted as well. Situated by the river, with a breeze blowing and fans set in strategic places, the heat was downright bearable. "The restaurant looks absolutely gorgeous."

"Thanks," Delilah said, looking pleased. "We were closed today so we could set up early and my staff has been here putting the final touches on everything while I was gone. We've been prepping the food for days. Have you eaten anything yet?"

"Not yet, but the food looks delicious." A long table with all kinds of hors d'oeuvres was set up against one of the walls inside while a matching table was set up across the room. "Those are unusual flower arrangements." The enormous arrangements, one for each buffet table, consisted of purple hyacinths, daffodils, blue irises, and red roses, with a little greenery added.

Delilah laughed. "Those are the kind of flowers Graham

sent Bella when he was trying to get her to forgive him."

"Forgive him? Oh, you mean when they broke up? I heard he sent a bunch of flowers to the shop."

"He did. Culminating in red roses when he proposed. He also sent cat toys for Bella's cat."

"Her cat?"

"Yes, Abby took a dislike to him but he won her over. Mostly by bribery."

They both laughed. "It sounds very romantic."

"Oh, it was."

Turner walked up just then. "Great job on the reception, Delilah."

"Thanks, Turner. Excuse me, I think I'm needed at the buffet."

"Let's dance," he said to Charlie and held out his hand. Most of the songs were fast and the crowd on the dance floor was suitably rowdy.

But when the music turned slow and Turner took her in his arms, she looked up to see an expression on his face that she couldn't decipher at first. Sad, she realized. "What are you thinking about that's making you sad?"

His expression cleared. "Not sad. Just thinking."

"About what?"

He looked down at her with a half-smile. "How much I like holding you in my arms."

"I like being here," she said without thinking.

He kissed her and said, "Are you ready to leave?"

"We can't leave yet. They haven't even cut the wedding cake."

"Damn. I guess you're right."

The whole affair was romantic, even more so than the previous wedding she'd attended with Turner. The intimate wedding ceremony with the couple's closest friends and family, the fairy-tale reception, and most of all, Graham and Bella's blissful happiness all contributed to a night that was the epitome of love and romance. It made her wistful, made her wish that she could have that happy ending. The one she'd once thought possible. She knew Graham and Bella, and had a fair idea of the problems they'd encountered on their way to their happy ending. Graham was divorced and by all accounts, his previous marriage had been one of his and Bella's main issues. But they'd worked their way through it. So it was possible.

Just not for her and Turner. No matter how much she wished it was.

TURNER COULDN'T PUT his finger on what was going on with Charlie, but something was. She'd been acting off since this morning, he realized. When she'd asked him about kids and he'd shot off his big mouth. He wondered again if she was pregnant but she'd sworn she wasn't and that she'd tell him. And Charlie wouldn't lie to him. Not about something like that.

Maybe he was just being paranoid. That could happen when you were crazy in love with a woman and you weren't sure how she felt about you. Life had been a lot simpler when he had thought he and Charlie were just friends. The fact that he'd never believed anyone she dated was worthy of her might have been a clue to his true feelings, but no, he'd been too dense to figure it out.

Turner lived in the same apartment building as Graham, in the Millennial Village apartments, which were next door to the hospital. He lived on one of the top floors facing Wisteria Lane, which gave him a beautiful view of the undeveloped land beyond the residential areas. He knew it would be commercialized at some point with residences or businesses or both, but he hoped it would be a while before that happened. In the meantime, he enjoyed looking at it.

His apartment was comfortable and it suited him. A dark brown leather couch, a matching armchair and a recliner, a pretty carved wood coffee table, and some side tables completed his den. He had a dining room table, which he considered useless, since he rarely cooked and wouldn't subject his company to it anyway. He usually ate at the kitchen bar.

He had eclectic tastes, so the artwork he'd collected ran from works of Gabe Walker—the well-known metal artist from Whiskey River—to work by obscure artists that he chanced upon during the local festivals, in Last Stand restaurants that hosted local artists' work, or when he traveled. His only requirement was that he liked it.

He loosened his tie, took it off and tossed it on the countertop. "Can I get you something to drink?"

Charlie had been staring at one of Gabe's masterpieces, one he called simply, "Midnight," but at that she turned around and smiled at him. "Water would be good."

He took a couple of bottles from the refrigerator and gave her one. He opened his, drank, and said, "You've been awfully quiet since we left the reception. Did something happen that upset you?"

"No, not at all. It was a beautiful wedding and reception. Graham and Bella look very happy."

"Yeah." He laughed a little. "I wasn't sure they'd ever get there, though. I don't think Graham came to terms with his divorce until after he met Bella."

"Divorce isn't an easy thing to come to terms with."

"Have you?" He winced. Damn, why had he mentioned that? "Sorry."

"Why? It's a legitimate question." She put her water down and sat on the couch. "He was the one to file. I was—I guess you could say I was blindsided."

He waited but she didn't elaborate. "Did you love him?"

"At first. But by the time he filed, I don't know what I felt."

"You've never talked about it to me."

"I've never talked about it to anyone except Audrey."

That made sense. He knew how close she was to her sister. "I'm glad you had someone you can trust."

Consternation flooded her face. "Turner, it doesn't mean I don't trust you."

Seemed that way to him. "If you think I'd pass judgment on you—"

"No, of course I don't. I know you wouldn't."

"You think I won't understand." Maybe he wouldn't,

since he had no idea what the problem was.

She rose and crossed the room to where he stood by the kitchen. Taking his hand, she said, "I think you would understand. But I'm not ready to talk about it."

He searched her face. "Then we won't. There are a lot more pleasant things we could do."

Too much to hope she'd open up to him any more. Not about her marriage. She'd already opened up more in the last few minutes than she had at any time since she came back to Last Stand. He put his hands on her waist and drew her close, then leaned down and kissed the line of her jaw. Kept going until he reached her ear.

"I like the way you think," she said.

He kissed her mouth, thrusting his tongue inside to meet hers. Then he picked her up and carried her into his bedroom. She went to work on his shirt buttons and by the time they reached the bed, she had most of them undone. Once there, she turned her back to him so he could unzip her dress. He placed kisses on her nape, unzipping her slowly and following the opening with his lips until he reached the small of her back. She let her dress fall and stepped out of it as he shrugged off his shirt and started on his pants.

Charlie turned around and helped him out of the rest of his clothes. Soon they were both naked. They kissed, his hands on her breasts, kneading them. Kissed more, hungry, demanding kisses. He boosted her up with her legs around him and laid her back on the bed.

He drew back slightly and just looked at her, thinking how beautiful she was and how lucky he was that he could be with her.

"Hurry," she told him hoarsely.

He didn't need urging. He pulled her to the edge of the bed and spread her legs wide before entering her with a solid, driving thrust. She wrapped her legs around his hips and met him thrust for thrust. He drove in and pulled back, slowly at first, then faster and faster until he pushed inside her one last time and came with a rush that nearly blew off the top of his head. Moments later, he felt her tighten around him and spasm, and she came in one long, shuddering orgasm.

Collapsing beside her on the bed, he rolled onto his back and pulled her on top of him. Took her face in his hands and kissed her. "I love you," he said. "So much."

Charlie froze.

Oh, shit, did I say that out loud?

Chapter Fourteen

CHARLIE ROLLED OFF of him, sat up and stared at him. *What am I supposed to do now? Turner said he loved me. Which means…what?*

He sat up too, looking chagrined.

Maybe he hadn't meant it.

"Crap. I didn't mean to say that."

She breathed a little easier. "Why? Because you don't?"

"No, I do. But I knew you'd freak out so I wasn't planning on telling you."

Charlie got out of bed. Rather than putting her dress back on, she picked up Turner's tux shirt and put that on. She turned her back to him, carefully buttoning the buttons, while she tried to think what to say. What to do. She turned around. "There are things you don't know about me that will change our relationship."

"There's nothing you could say that would change the way I feel about you."

"You don't know that."

"Neither do you, since you haven't told me what these things are that are supposed to 'change our relationship,'" he said, making air quotes.

She began to pace. "This is exactly what I was afraid would happen."

"What? Falling in love?"

"Yes, damn it. I knew I shouldn't have agreed to date you. We should have stayed friends and not complicated things." She glanced at him as she walked. He was sitting on the bed—naked—which did not help matters at all. "You need to put on some clothes."

He had the nerve to grin at her. "I don't think so."

"If you think I'm going to fall back in bed with you, think again."

"Okay. So why do you care if I'm dressed or not?"

"Because you're distracting me, damn it!"

He laughed but he grabbed his boxers and put them on. "There. Better?"

Not really. "This isn't funny, Turner."

"I can see that you think it's not. Why is this such a surprise to you? You had to at least have had a clue I was falling for you."

"I hoped I was wrong."

"Why?"

She shook her head. "We need to break up."

He stared at her. "You want to break up because I'm in love with you."

"It's for the best."

"You realize this makes no sense, right?"

She had to tell him. Now before it went any further.

"I know you care about me," he said.

"Of course I do. But I can't fall in love again." Which

was absurd, because she was definitely in love with Turner.

He took her hand and pulled her toward the bed. "Sit down. Tell me what's going on, Charlie."

She drew in a breath. "If we stay together you'll want to commit ourselves to each other. You'll want to marry and have a family."

"I hadn't gotten that far, especially since I wasn't sure of your feelings, but yeah, that's the likely scenario. Eventually."

Her eyes filled with tears. "I can't give you a family. I can't give you a child." There, it was out. Her tears fell more freely.

"That's not something we need to decide immediately, is it? Can't we talk about it?"

"No. It won't make a difference. I had a hysterectomy. I can't ever have children. I can't give you a child of your own, Turner."

He simply looked at her for a moment, then put his arms around her and held her close. She laid her head against his chest, wishing she could stay that way forever. "I'm so sorry."

"Me too." She sniffled and pulled away from him. "So now you see why we have to break up."

"No, I don't. I don't see that your ability or inability to have children makes a damn bit of difference to us."

"Oh, Turner, of course it will. Maybe not right now, but later. The more involved we get, the worse it will be when we finally do break up."

"If marriage is what's freaking you out, you can relax. I promise I won't ask you to marry me."

Her eyes filled with tears that she struggled to hold back. "Take me home, Turner. We can't do this. I can't do it. It isn't fair to you."

"Screw that. I don't care. I just want to be with you. And don't deny that's what you want too because I won't believe you." He put his arm around her. "Look, I know you're upset. I get that. But you don't need to leave. Let's take some time and think about this. We'll talk in the morning. For now, let's just be together."

Looking into his eyes, she hesitated. She didn't want to leave him at all. But she couldn't string him along. It wouldn't be fair. "I won't change my mind," she repeated. "But if you want me to stay, for tonight, I will."

"I want you to stay," he said.

She got up and walked over to lay her dress on the back of a chair. As she returned, she unbuttoned his shirt. When she reached the bed, she took it off. If she was going to allow herself one last night, she wanted it to be memorable. She straddled his lap and kissed him and tried to put everything out of her mind except now, this moment with Turner.

I shouldn't have stayed, she thought in the early morning hours after they'd made love again and again. One long night of lovemaking to last for a lifetime. Maybe she didn't have to break up with him. Maybe they could simply continue the way they were and pretend he'd never said those fateful words.

Every day you wait will make the inevitable that much harder. And you know it's inevitable.

That very morning Turner had proven what he really

thought about having kids—when a mother and child had entered the shop. And when she questioned him later about wanting children, he'd said, "Sure." As if it were no big deal.

But it was a big deal. A very big deal.

TURNER WOKE UP before Charlie. Not wanting to wake her, he didn't move, but used the time to simply study her face. To engrave her beautiful face in his memory. Because he was afraid he knew what would happen later. She would insist they had to break up.

How was he supposed to convince her that her having a child wasn't a problem for him? He understood why she was upset. He even got why she'd think it might matter to him. But the bottom line was, it didn't.

Charlie opened her eyes. For a moment she smiled at him. Then her smile faded and her eyes filled with tears.

"We don't have to break up," he said, though he knew just from looking at her that she would continue to argue.

"Yes, we do."

"If you think you're doing this for me, think again."

"It's the best thing for both of us. We're only going to grow closer and that will make it even harder when we end things."

He sat up and ran his hands through his hair. "I need coffee. And then we'll talk."

"All right. But there's no point talking."

There damn sure is. What in the hell had happened with

her ex? Something had made her feel as if her childbearing abilities were the only thing that mattered. When she was so much more than that.

Charlie got out of bed, gathered her clothes together and went into the bathroom. Turner got up and put on his jeans and a T-shirt. He went to the kitchen and made coffee, trading places with Charlie when she came out of the bathroom.

He walked into the den and saw that Charlie was sitting on the couch with two steaming mugs of coffee on the table in front of her.

"I don't want to break up."

"It's what has to happen."

"Because I'm in love with you."

"Yes."

"Because you can't have children."

"Yes," she repeated. "I won't do that to you."

"First of all, why are we talking about marriage, much less kids? I told you last night I wouldn't ask you to marry me." Even though he realized that was exactly what he wanted. "Do you really think that whether or not you can have a child matters one damn bit to me? There are plenty of other ways to have children, you know."

"It mattered to my ex-husband. It's the reason he walked out on me."

"What? He left you because—"

"Because I couldn't have children. His children." She nodded and looked so hurt, his heart broke. "That's why we divorced."

Damn. No wonder she thought he'd care. She'd already had one man—more of a turd than a man—reject her because she couldn't have his biological children.

"Tell me what happened."

"I guess I should start from the first. I met Lance Archer in Los Angeles when we both entered a competition for a cooking show. He was good. Really good. And really good-looking. All the women wanted him but he ignored them. He made it very clear he was interested in me. Only me. I was flattered."

She closed her eyes and shook her head. "After the competition was over—he won, but I placed second—we started seeing each other. He was charming. Personable. Supportive. We had the same interests. Our careers complemented each other. I concentrated on pies and pastries, his thing was entrees.

"I'm ashamed to say I fell for his looks. But he treated me well. He was so sweet and considerate. My friends thought he was great. And he was great. Until he wasn't.

"We'd been married about a year. I wanted a baby, desperately. But Lance wouldn't hear of it. He wasn't ready, a baby would be too expensive, the two of us were fine so why add anyone to it, any excuse he could think of. I thought we had time. I still wanted a child but I didn't think there was any urgency to it. Then I started having problems."

"Gynecological problems," Turner said.

"You guessed it. I developed endometriosis and had to have a hysterectomy. Not long after that, before I'd even fully recovered, Lance walked out on me."

"Why?"

"Because he'd changed his mind. The minute he realized I couldn't give him a child of his own, that's what he wanted. So he left."

Unfreakingbelievable. "God, Charlie. I'm sorry. Bastard is too mild a term for him."

"It doesn't matter. I'm glad we're divorced. His timing sucked, though."

"His timing was cruel. I doubt it was coincidental. The bastard did it to hurt you."

"Maybe, but I think it was mostly because he had another woman in his sights. He could see I was devastated by the hysterectomy, but he didn't want to waste time on me. So he walked out."

"Charlie, just because one man walked out when you needed him most doesn't mean every man will."

"I know that. I do, Turner. But you're not thinking clearly. You need to think about this. Really think about what you want to do. I know you think you love me—"

"I don't think. I know I love you. I'm not a kid. I know my own mind."

"Are you going to deny that if we stay together, you'll eventually want to get married?"

"I don't see what that has to do with anything."

"Yes, you do. I asked you once if you wanted kids and you said, 'Sure.'"

"So? That doesn't mean I have to have a biological child. There's adoption."

"You think you'd be happy with that but you haven't

155

considered everything. You need to think, really think about your feelings." She stood. "Will you take me home?"

He didn't want to but what could he say? "All right. But we're not breaking up."

"Why are you being so stubborn? If you don't want to call it breaking up, fine. We're taking a break."

"What's the difference?"

"We won't see each other for two weeks. That should be long enough for you to think this through. Then, at the end of that time, you can tell me your decision. One you've really and truly thought about."

"And if I haven't changed my mind? If I still don't give a shit that you can't have my biological kids? What then?"

"We'll talk about it when the two weeks is up."

He wasn't the stubborn one here. But it was clearly useless to point that out.

Chapter Fifteen

"ARE YOU READY to admit you made a terrible mistake when you cut Turner loose?"

Charlie rolled her eyes. Audrey had cornered her during a lull, while she was prepping for the following day. Her sister always spoke her mind and she'd been doing that for the last week. "Give it a rest, Audrey. I didn't cut him loose. I simply gave him time to think."

"You're not giving him enough credit. If you two stay together and want kids, I'm sure he'd be open to adoption."

"I know. That's not the point." He'd said as much to her. But she didn't want him to regret a decision like that. She knew he wouldn't do what her ex had done. Turner was a good person, unlike Lance, who was a selfish prick. But knowing Turner yearned for something she couldn't give him would be unbearable for both of them.

The shop bells jangled. "You'd better go get that."

"You go. I'll put up the dough," Audrey said. "You need some human contact."

Rather than argue—and lose anyway—she went. *Tourist or new to town*, she thought when she saw the mid-thirties woman with a little girl of about five or six.

"Hi, how can I help you?"

"Hi. Your shop is so cute. And the word is the pies are to die for."

"Thank you. That's so nice to hear," she said with a smile. "Have you ladies decided on what kind of pie you'd like?"

"Chocolate," the little girl said. "A ginormous chocolate pie!"

"We'll have to ask your mom about that," Charlie told the child diplomatically.

"Definitely a big one," she said to Charlie with a wink. "And I'll have a slice of peach cobbler."

"Coming right up." She went to the back to get the chocolate pie out of the refrigerator and to heat up the cobbler.

When she returned with the pies, the woman put both pieces on the nearest table and told the child, "Aim for your mouth, honey. How much do I owe you?" she asked Charlie.

Charlie told her. Looking from one to the other, she said, "Your little girl looks just like you. She's adorable." They were both blond and blue eyed with curly hair, and the shape of their faces was similar as well.

The woman laughed. "Thank you. We get that a lot and it's so funny. Lacey is adopted."

"Oh, I had no idea." She sent a worried glance toward the little girl who was within earshot.

"Don't worry. Lacey knows all about how we ended up as a family. Don't you, sweetheart?" she asked her daughter.

"I'm special," Lacey announced, looking up from her pie

that was now all over her face. "Mommy and Daddy choosed me."

"That's wonderful. You're all very lucky," Charlie said.

"Yes, and what's even funnier is that we adopted Lacey at birth, so we had no idea she'd grow up to look so much like me." She smiled at her daughter fondly. "Did we, pumpkin?"

Lacey shook her head, curls bouncing.

"I'm Tina Grier," she said, offering her hand. "We recently moved to Whiskey River so you'll be seeing us again. The rumors were true. Your pie is delicious."

"Charlie Stockton," she said, shaking hands. "My sister Audrey and I own the shop."

They left a short while later, after Tina, as she put it, "hosed off" Lacey, who, even so, wore a good bit of pie when she left.

Charlie turned the sign in the door to Closed after Tina and Lacey left. In her head, she knew she'd love any child she adopted. Could she deny that Turner would too? Or had Lance's reaction to her hysterectomy so damaged her that she couldn't believe any man would truly want a child who wasn't his own? But Turner wasn't just any man. She had no doubt he would love an adopted child. The question was, would he ever regret not having his biological child?

"What in the world are you thinking about?" Audrey said. "I've been trying to get your attention for the last five minutes."

"Oh, sorry. I was just thinking about what we need to do for tomorrow." She *should* have been thinking about it, anyway.

159

"Nothing. We're ready to go. And you and I are in dire need of relaxation."

"We are?"

"Yes. Come with me."

"I can't—"

"Yes, you can," Audrey said, taking her arm. "We're going to the Saloon and we're going to have a drink and you're going to talk to me. About you and Turner."

"There's no point in talking. Turner is thinking things over. I said we wouldn't see each other until he's had time to do that."

"If this is about your ex—"

"Of course it is, to some extent. Audrey, you don't get it. You've never had a failed marriage. You can't imagine how that eats away at your self-confidence."

"I don't think your self-confidence is suffering. I think it's your loss of faith in men—all men—that's the issue."

Maybe it was. Which would be stupid, since Turner had never done anything to make her question her faith in him. Not once. How many people could you say that about?

"You're totally in love with him," Audrey continued. "It's past time you admitted it and did something about it."

"You don't understand."

"Explain it to me."

Charlie pulled away and paced. "He needs time to think before he ties himself down with a woman who can't have his children. He told me he loved me, Audrey. What the hell was I supposed to do?"

"Gee, I don't know. Say, I love you too, throw yourself

into his arms and live happily ever after?"

If only I could. "I can't."

"Even though you want to."

"Yes."

"Even though you love him."

"Damn it, yes."

Audrey shook her head. "You're not making any sense at all. Come on," she said, and grabbed Charlie's hand to pull her along. "We're going to the Saloon."

My God, her sister was stubborn. Charlie sighed and gave in. She wasn't doing anything useful here at the shop. Besides, Audrey would just hound her until she went with her.

"I'll go but I don't want to talk about Turner."

"We'll see about that."

)⚶≪

"WHAT WILL YOU have?" Slater Highwater asked Turner as he slid a cardboard coaster toward him.

"A draft. Thanks, Slater."

"I'll have the same," Spencer said. To Turner he said, "What do you mean you don't want to play pool? We always play pool at the Saloon."

"I'm not in the mood," he said, taking the beer Slater had just served him and gulping some down. He hadn't wanted to come at all, but his little brother had nagged the shit out of him until he agreed.

"You've been a real pain in the ass since you and Charlie

broke up, you know that?"

"Go to hell," he said, without heat. A man should be able to be a pain in the ass when the woman he loved was being completely unreasonable. "Besides, we're taking a break. It's not the same as breaking up." He hoped.

"Uh-huh. That's code for breaking up."

"Really?" He chugged some beer. "I had no idea." He wished he could talk to someone—one of his brothers, or Jessie or his parents—but he didn't feel comfortable talking about something that Charlie had told him in confidence. Though she hadn't specifically said not to tell anyone, the fact that only he and Audrey knew about her hysterectomy made it clear she wanted it kept confidential.

"Don't look now but guess who just walked in?"

He didn't need to look to know who Spencer was referring to; nevertheless, he did. Charlie, naturally. Standing in the doorway with her sister, looking as beautiful as ever in an old, tight pair of jeans and a T-shirt with "Pilates? I thought you said Pie and Lattes" inscribed on it. He'd only seen her from a distance since she'd told him she wanted to take a break. Probably because he hadn't been anywhere except the hospital, his own apartment and on short trips into town when necessary until tonight.

Charlie looked at the bar and saw him. He knew she saw him because she gave a half-hearted wave and immediately turned away. This was stupid. He wasn't going to change his mind. Did she really think his love for her was so fragile that he'd give up on her simply because she couldn't have kids? He finished off his beer and stood. Apparently she did believe that. So he was going to set her straight.

"Turner, what are you doing?" Spencer asked him.

"I'm going over to tell her I'm done with this taking a break crap," he said grimly.

"Good luck," Spencer said. The "you're going to need it" was implied.

He walked up to their table. "Hi, Audrey. Charlie. Mind if I sit down?"

Charlie's expression was so horrified, he almost laughed. Except it wasn't funny. Not one damn bit.

"Please, sit," Audrey said. "I'll just go get us those drinks, Charlie." She left but not before giving Turner a significant look and mouthing, "Good luck."

Why did everyone think he needed luck?

Because you do.

"We've been *taking a break* for over a week now."

"I know."

"I've missed you." He probably shouldn't say it but screw it.

"I've missed you, too."

"Then why are we putting ourselves through this?" He laid his hand on top of hers. "I'm not going to change my mind, Charlie."

She let her hand stay where it was. "You haven't had enough time to think about it."

"Yes, I have. And another thing. Why are you acting as if we're going to get married immediately? Are you ready to get married?"

"No."

"Neither am I." *Liar. You've been ready to marry her since*

163

the moment you realized you loved her, and probably have for a long time. "It's not as if I asked you to marry me. Why are we worrying about what *might* happen in some unknowable future?"

"Because the longer we stay together, the harder it will be when we break up."

"Don't you mean *if* we break up?" He gazed at her, understanding dawning slowly. "Now I see it. You're convinced we won't stay together, aren't you? Because of your shithead ex-husband. You think I'll change my mind, like he did."

"I didn't say that."

"You didn't need to. It's written all over your face. The bottom line is you don't trust me."

"That's not true. Of course I trust you."

"Maybe about some things. But not about this. You don't trust me to know my own mind or to be honest with you. You don't know me at all." Hell, no wonder she'd been so insistent that he think things over. She was letting him down easy.

"Turner, I do trust you. It's just that—"

"Oh, I know what it is. You're hoping I'll change my mind so you don't have to be the one to call things off. Why don't you be honest and tell me you don't trust me and don't want to be with me?"

Her eyes were bright with unshed tears. Another time, he would have felt like a jerk making her cry, but right now he was too pissed and upset to be mindful of that. "I'll save you the trouble." He stood.

"What does that mean?" she asked him.

"It means we're done."

Chapter Sixteen

IT MEANS WE'RE done.

Turner's words echoed in Charlie's mind, as they had every day and night of the last week since she'd seen him at the Saloon. God, she wished she could forget that night. The pain in his eyes when he'd realized she didn't trust him.

Because he was right. She admitted it now. She was afraid to let things play out with Turner. Afraid of what would happen if sometime down the road, he changed his mind.

She'd dreamed of having a baby since she was a child herself. After she married Lance, the longing had become intense. She'd wanted a baby. To carry a child, to feel the miracle of nurturing the baby inside of her. Then the dream had died. And she'd been shattered.

Yet instead of pulling herself together and getting on with her life, she'd allowed Lance and what he'd done to keep her in stasis, believing every man would disappoint her if she opened herself up again.

Turner had blown through all her defenses as only a man who knew her inside and out could. Once he'd decided he wanted her, it had been inevitable that she would fall in love with him. Because she knew him as well as he knew her. And she *knew* he was entirely trustworthy. Yet she hadn't trusted him.

She didn't blame him for breaking up with her. She'd hurt him badly and he didn't deserve it. Why had it taken him breaking up with her before she realized how unhappy she was without him and how much she wanted another chance? *Because you're a stubborn fool convinced you were doing the right thing for Turner when it was always yourself you were worried about.*

The problem was, she had no idea how to go about asking him for another chance. Or even if he had any desire to give her another chance.

Late that evening she got a call. She nearly didn't answer since it wasn't a ringtone she knew but she checked and saw Jameson Hospital on the caller ID. *This can't be good.*

"Hello. Who's this?"

"It's Graham McBride, Charlie. I thought you'd want to know that Turner was in a car accident tonight."

Her stomach plummeted. "Is he all right? Where is he? What happened?"

"I don't know anything yet, other than that he's en route to the hospital. I'm here waiting for him. The accident happened just outside of town."

Oh, God. Her heart had stopped at Graham's first words. Now it slammed against her ribs in a slow, painful thump. "He's not..." She couldn't say it. But Graham would have told her if... "He's...he's...alive?"

"Yes. Sorry, I should have told you that first thing. But I

don't know how serious it is. I can let you know when he gets here and I find out more."

"I'm coming there," she said and hung up.

Ten minutes later, she walked into the ER waiting room. There were only a few people there. Most seemed to be waiting for someone to see them. She didn't see Graham or Spencer and went to the desk to ask about Turner.

"Is Dr. Turner McBride here? As a patient, I mean."

"Yes, he just came in. Are you family?"

"No. No…I'm a…friend." Which she was, even if he didn't ever want to see her again. And she couldn't blame him for that, either. "Are his brothers here? Or any of his family?"

"Yes, his brothers are with him now."

"If you see one of them could you tell them Charlie's here and ask if they'd come talk to me?"

"Yes. Are you all right, ma'am? You look like you're going to pass out."

"I'm fine. Just worried."

She took a seat and waited. And while she waited, she replayed in her mind every word of their last conversation, every expression on his face. She thought about how their relationship had changed after the Cancer Society fund-raiser. She remembered every time they made love, every time he'd made her laugh, every time they'd done nothing but be content to be around each other. If she got the chance, she would tell him she knew what a fool she'd been and how she regretted making him feel as if she didn't trust him.

Charlie looked at the clock on the wall again. Four minutes after the last time she looked. Why hadn't Graham come out to talk to her? He'd called her to let her know about the accident. Surely he'd realize how frantic she was. Or would he? He knew she and Turner had broken up. Maybe he'd only called because...Oh, God, what if it was worse than the desk clerk had let on?

"WHAT THE HELL do you mean you called Mom and Dad?" Turner said. "I've got a broken arm. I'm not dying. I don't need the whole fam-damily here." He sat on the gurney in the exam area, a cubicle divided by cloth curtains, waiting to hear the results of his tests. The paramedics, not Spencer but someone else, had put his arm in a vacuum splint, immobilized it and stuck some Steri-Strips on the cuts on his face. Though the X-ray techs had unwrapped him—thank God because he'd felt like a burrito—they were able to x-ray him through the splint. He'd also had his ribs x-rayed and a head CT. He wasn't worried about either of those results. He figured he'd know if something was wrong.

Graham and Spencer exchanged a look. "I'd bet money you broke some ribs as well," Spencer said. "Besides, I'm not risking Mom's wrath just because you're grumpy. Not to mention Jessie's."

He probably did have broken ribs, if the pain was anything to go by. They hadn't given him any pain meds yet and wouldn't until the results of the tests were in. He'd been pretty out of it when they'd pulled him out of his car, but he suspected his 'vette was in really bad shape. Damn it, why hadn't he taken the SUV? On top of worrying about his car, who knew how long it would be before he could operate again? He'd seen the X-ray and didn't need a radiologist's diagnosis to know his arm was broken.

Spencer looked at Graham. "You can tell him. I told him about Mom and Dad."

"Tell me what? When the hell will I get the results?"

"It's the ER. You know how this goes."

Of course he did. But it didn't make him happy. Something else that didn't make him happy were his brothers. Graham was looking way too guilty. Turner narrowed his eyes at him. "What did you do?"

Graham shrugged. "I called Charlie and told her you'd been in an accident."

"Why the hell did you do that? We broke up, remember?"

"She needed to know. In fact, she's probably out in the waiting room right now."

Great. Just great. He had a splitting headache. His ribs and arm hurt like a bitch. He was not up for seeing Charlie, assuming she'd even come. "I doubt she's there."

"I'll go see. Want me to bring her back if she is?"

"No. Yes. Shit, I don't know."

Graham went out, leaving him with Spencer who, naturally, had to give Turner his opinion. "You and Charlie should get back together."

"Thanks, oh wise one. In case you've forgotten what I

told you after I saw her at the Saloon, she doesn't trust me. She thinks I'll treat her like her ex did. If she can't trust me—someone she's known basically her entire life—"

Spencer interrupted. "What did her ex do to her? Was he abusive?"

"Not in the sense you mean. But he did a number on her self-esteem."

"Charlie doesn't act like she has low self-esteem."

"Most of the time she doesn't. But when she found out—" He cut himself off before he said too much. "Her ex is a lot of the reason she questions me and what we could have."

"Does she still have feelings for him?"

"Yeah. I'm fairly sure she hates his guts."

"Well that's good, isn't it?"

Turner started to shrug and cursed instead. "I don't want to talk about Charlie."

"Okay. Do you know how the accident happened?" Spencer asked.

Well, it was a change of subject, even if it wasn't one he wanted to dwell on either. "Not exactly. I was driving down the road coming back from Austin and the next thing I knew, the truck coming toward me veered into my lane, hit me on the driver's side and shoved my car off the road into a ditch. Boom, the airbags deployed and I was stuck until EMS came." He grimaced and added, "It happened without warning so I couldn't even dodge. I guess I should be glad he didn't hit me head-on. The asshole was probably texting."

"Ding, ding, ding. That's what the cops thought. His cell

phone was on, open to messages, and lying beside him. He didn't have a scratch on him, by the way."

"Typical," Turner muttered. "Do you know what happened to my car? How bad is it?"

"It's been towed. You probably don't want to know how much damage was done until you have to."

Oh, hell, he'd been afraid of that.

"Graham talked to the orthopedist. He should be in soon."

"Whatever." Very carefully, he lay back down. Closed his eyes and tried not to think about the wreck and his poor car. Or how long it would be before he could operate again. Or how much every freaking bone in his body hurt. And he especially didn't want to think about Charlie. What was the point?

CHARLIE JUMPED UP when she saw Graham walk into the waiting room. She couldn't decipher his expression but surely he'd look more upset if something was horribly wrong. "How is he?"

"He'll be all right. He's pretty banged up but he'll heal. He's got a broken arm and broken ribs but all in all, he was lucky."

Broken arm? Broken ribs? That didn't sound lucky to her. "Can I see him? Does he know I'm here? Does he know you called me?"

Graham nodded. "I told him you were probably out here

waiting."

"He doesn't want to see me, does he?"

"Honestly, Charlie, I'm not sure he knows what he wants. He's in a lot of pain and hasn't had any pain medicine yet." Graham hesitated, then said, "He still loves you, you know."

"I hurt him. That was the last thing I wanted to do."

"Do you love him?"

She nodded miserably. "Yes."

"I don't know what the problem is with you two. But I almost let go of the best thing that ever happened to me, and trust me, you don't want to do that. Thank God I realized that in time to convince Bella to give me another chance. If Turner screwed up—"

"He didn't. He didn't do anything wrong. This is all on me."

"It's rarely one person's fault."

"What about you and Bella? You basically said that was all your fault."

He gave a wry smile. "Yes, but that time, it really was. Besides, I said rarely."

"Turner thinks I don't trust him. But that's not true."

"You'll have to convince him you do."

How? How did she convince Turner that she loved and trusted him?

He patted her arm. "You'll figure it out. Sounds like you two need to talk. He's in exam cubicle two, waiting for test results and to get another splint."

"Thank you. Thank you for calling me."

"I thought you needed to know." He looked toward the entrance and said, "There's the rest of the family. I'll give them an update while you go see Turner."

"Thanks," she repeated.

The curtain was partially open and Charlie could see Spencer sitting in a chair. She pulled aside the curtain and peeked inside. Turner lay on his back with his eyes closed. "Graham said I could come back," she told Spencer.

At the sound of her voice Turner opened his eyes.

"I wasn't sure you'd want to see me," she said to him.

"I'll be back," Spencer said. He looked at Turner and gave him a thumbs-up before he left.

"I always want to see you."

She sighed in relief and walked over to stand beside the gurney. She slipped her hand into his uninjured hand. "I was really scared when I heard about your accident."

"Graham shouldn't have called you. I'm fine."

"Yes, you look just great."

"Considering the probable state of my car, I do."

"Your Corvette?"

"Yeah. I think it's totaled."

She knew how much he loved that car. "I'm sorry, Turner."

He didn't say anything, but shifted and pulled his hand away to put it on his chest above the temporary splint.

She tamped down her disappointment. After all, she knew this wouldn't be easy. "Graham told me you have a broken arm and broken ribs. Do you have a concussion?"

"I don't think so. I never lost consciousness. But I have a

devil of a headache."

"Do you know what happened?"

"A pickup ran into me. Texting and driving, they think."

"Oh, my God. That's so scary. I'm glad you weren't hurt worse."

"Me too." He started to sit up but it obviously caused him a lot of pain, so he subsided. "Charlie, why are you here?"

"I had to make sure you were okay. I had no idea how badly you were hurt."

"As you can see, I'm not going to die," he said with a bite to his words.

So much for him being glad to see her. He was angry with her and she couldn't blame him. "Do you want me to leave?"

"I don't know." Then, "No."

She drew in a breath and said, "I've missed you. I hate not seeing you. But this is a crappy time to talk about us."

"Talk about us? What's there to talk about? You don't trust me. You've known me for years, we've been friends since we were kids. But you don't trust me not to do what your ex did. You don't trust me to know my own mind. Period, end of discussion."

"I do trust you." He didn't say anything. She couldn't tell if that was because he truly was finished with her or he felt too shitty to talk about it, which was probably true, no matter if he was done with her or not. "We can talk later. This was a stupid time to try to discuss anything."

"True, but you brought it up. Spell it out for me, Charlie. What are you trying to say?"

"I love you."

Turner stared at her. "What did you say?"

"I said I love you."

A doctor came in just then and said, "Let's see about that broken arm, Turner."

Charlie left him with the doctor.

Chapter Seventeen

TURNER WAS NEVER sure how it happened, but Charlie drove him home from the hospital. He was still reeling from her admission…unless he'd hallucinated it, which was entirely possible. Once at his place, she not only didn't leave but she stayed and "got him settled" in bed with pillows propping him up, and pain pills and water on the bedside table. He didn't argue with her. The pain pills had kicked in by then and all he wanted to do was sleep.

When he woke up some time later, he saw Charlie was still there, sitting in the easy chair in his bedroom. Actually, it was the chair he threw his clothes on but she'd apparently taken care of those. "Why are you here?"

"Oh, good, you're awake. I'll go heat up some soup for you."

"I don't have any soup."

"You do now. In fact, you have a lot more than just soup. I went to the store for you."

He glanced at the clock on the bedside table. "It's the middle of the night. Why are you still here?"

"Because you need someone to take care of you."

"No, I don't. I'll be fine." To prove it, he decided he had

to use the bathroom and tried to get out of bed. Charlie was right beside him.

"I can pee by myself," he told her irritably.

"Good, because I'm not helping with that. But I'm walking you to the bathroom. You're not very steady right now."

Turner thought with disgust that he was too weak to argue. He shuffled along with Charlie hanging on to his good arm. He couldn't decide whether his ribs or his arm hurt more. He decided it was a draw. Damned if she wasn't waiting for him when he finished. He scowled at her but let her hold his good arm again and lead him back to bed.

"I'm staying and I'm taking care of you, so you might as well get over it. There's no way you can kick me out, you know."

Too tired and befuddled to argue, he got in bed and went back to sleep. A little while later, Charlie woke him to eat some soup and crackers. Which he had to admit made him feel better. He drank some water, took another pain pill, went back to sleep and when he woke again, it was morning. Charlie was asleep in the chair. He made it to the bathroom on his own, did his business, brushed his teeth, sponged off, none of which was a pleasant task. When he came out, she was awake and fluffing his pillows and straightening the sheets and blanket.

"Shouldn't you be at work?"

"It's Sunday."

"Oh." He'd forgotten that. "Still, I'm sure you have better things to do. I don't need a babysitter."

She tilted her head and said, "Now where have I heard

that before? Oh, I know. I said it to you, and you told me I *did* need a babysitter. Something about not realizing I had a serious injury."

He started to argue but since he still felt pretty shitty, and exhausted from cleaning up, he gave up. He would have shrugged if it hadn't hurt.

"I'll go make coffee."

"Thanks." He leaned back against the pillows. Six weeks until he got the cast off. Probably at least that long for the ribs to heal. That meant at the minimum, eight to ten weeks before he could operate. Maybe more. Damn, he'd have to send his upcoming surgeries, those that couldn't be put off, to another neurosurgeon. Plus, he'd need to line up someone to take call for him. He'd be able to see his patients for follow-ups and perhaps the initial diagnosis, but if they needed surgery, he'd have to send them elsewhere.

Shit.

"Here's your coffee," Charlie said, entering the room. "I can make you some toast and jelly too. But you might want to eat that in the other room, if you feel like sitting somewhere else for a while."

"I probably should. Let me drink some coffee first." He took a sip and studied her over the rim of the mug. "Not that I don't appreciate the help but I can take care of myself now."

"You took care of me after my concussion. It seems only right I should return the favor."

"Is that the only reason?"

"No. I told you yesterday. Don't you remember?"

"You mean when you said you loved me?"

"Yes."

He drank more coffee and set down the mug. "I wondered if I'd imagined that."

"You didn't. I love you, Turner. I've been miserable ever since you said we were done. No, before that. Since I told you we were taking a break."

He looked at her silently for a long moment. Yeah. He'd bet his last dollar she was reacting to his accident. And he didn't want that to be her reason for getting back together.

"You look like you don't believe me."

Because he didn't. "Do you want to know what I think? What I honestly think?"

"Of course."

"I think you're overreacting because my accident shook you up. It's a little suspicious that you didn't figure out you 'loved' me or wanted to be with me until after I was in an accident and might have been badly hurt. Or even killed."

"You have broken bones. Which is badly hurt in my book. But that's beside the point. I knew I loved you before that."

He wished he could believe that but he didn't. "Even if you do, nothing has changed. You still don't trust me."

She came over and sat on the edge of the bed beside him. "Yes, I do. But I don't know how to convince you of that."

Part of him wanted to accept what she said at face value. But the other part, the realist part of him, knew better. "I'm not sure you can."

BE PATIENT. YOU can't expect him to believe you immediately.
He was looking pale and drawn. He needed pain medicine
and some food. She shouldn't be arguing with him. Maybe
once he felt better, he'd listen to her. Believe her. But in the
meantime, he needed someone to take care of him. "We can
talk about all this later. Now is obviously not the time."

"Ya think?" He closed his eyes and leaned back, grimac-
ing when he did so.

"I'm sorry. I shouldn't have brought up any of this. Let's
just forget it until another time when you're not hurting so
much. Should I bring your food in here or do you feel like
coming into the other room?"

He opened his eyes. "I'll come in there. You go ahead.
I'll be there in a minute." She hesitated and he added,
sharply, "I didn't break my leg. I can walk on my own
without you hovering over me."

She swallowed her retort because he was right. She was
hovering. But damn, the man was stubborn. He needed her
help and she wasn't going to let him drive her away by being
grumpy. She was made of stronger stuff than that.

He came in a little while later and took a seat at the bar.
"Sorry I snapped at you."

"Don't worry about it. I've been snapped at before. I
know you're hurting." She set a plate in front of him laden
with eggs, bacon, toast and jelly. Which she knew was one of
his favorite meals. "More coffee or would you like milk?"

"Milk, please. Thanks. This is really good. I was hungrier

than I thought."

They didn't talk anymore. Not about anything important. He slept a lot for the rest of the day. Charlie gave him soup and sandwiches for lunch, then made a couple of casseroles so he would have leftovers he could easily heat up. She had a feeling he wasn't going to let her stay with him much longer.

"Thanks for making dinner," Turner said after she served them both one of the casseroles. "You didn't have to do that."

"I wanted to. I made you another one too. I froze half of each one. That way you'll have some ready-made dinners."

"Thanks. You don't need to stay with me tonight. I appreciate what you've done but I'm fine now."

He wasn't fine but he obviously wanted to fend for himself. Or he simply wanted her gone. "All right. I'll go home after I clean up from dinner. But call me if you need anything."

"I won't."

He moved to the couch and flipped on the TV. Charlie took her time cleaning up but eventually she finished. Turner was watching some kind of drama with lots of violence, something he knew she'd detest.

"You don't have to watch the goriest show you can find. Don't worry, I'm leaving."

"That's not why I'm watching it."

She raised an eyebrow. "If you say so. When do you get your regular cast on?"

"A couple more days if he thinks the swelling is down

enough." He muted the TV and got up. "Thanks for the food and everything."

"You're welcome." Oh, my God, they sounded like two strangers. Now was not the time to try to talk to him about the two of them. He'd made that perfectly clear. "Let me know if you need anything," she said again. Totally unnecessarily.

"Go home, Charlie. I'll be fine."

What could she do but leave? She heard the door shut and the lock click behind her. Apparently, she was an idiot. Had she really thought she could say, "Gee, I do trust you after all. Let's get back together," and Turner would fall into her arms? That all would be forgiven when she'd hurt him as badly as she had? Did he really believe that she only wanted him back because of the accident? Yes, knowing he could have been hurt, or worse, had been the impetus, but that didn't mean her feelings weren't genuine.

How in the hell was she going to convince Turner of that?

TURNER THOUGHT THE next few days would never end. Charlie came over after work every day. He tried, half-heartedly, to get her to stop, but she ignored him. She brought him pie. She cooked more food. She tried to wash his clothes until he forbade her to touch them. She might think she was proving to him that her sudden "love" for him was real instead of all about his accident, but if so, she was wrong.

It was killing him to see her. Killing him to wonder if she really did love him. But it was too damn coincidental. Just because he wanted her to love him didn't mean she did. Worse, he still couldn't believe she trusted him. No, she thought he'd regret it if they couldn't have kids "of their own." When that was the last thing he cared about. Sure, he wanted kids. But they didn't need to have his DNA for him to love them.

He'd had all he could take. The evening after he got his cast he decided it was time to put an end to this torture.

As usual, Charlie came over after work. With pie, of course. He let her in and stood by the door while she put the pie on the counter. She had a key but she always knocked and let him answer the door.

"Key lime tonight," Charlie said. "Want me to put it in the refrigerator?"

"No, leave it."

She glanced at him. "You got your cast."

"Yeah."

"Why are you standing there with the door open?"

"I'm waiting to show you out."

She looked puzzled. "What? Why?"

"Because it's time. I'm not an invalid. I'm going back to work tomorrow. I can still see patients even if I can't operate. So, thanks for all your help. I do appreciate it. But you need to leave."

"You're kicking me out? For…for good?"

"Look, Charlie, you don't need to take care of me. I'm

perfectly capable of taking care of myself. You've assuaged your conscience of whatever it is you thought you were doing. We're not together. We both have to get on with our lives. Separately."

Oh, shit, she's gonna cry. But she didn't, thank God.

She sucked in a breath and squared her shoulders. "I suppose you want your key back."

"Up to you. Here's yours," he said, handing her his key to her house.

Charlie took the key off her keychain and handed it to him. "I hope your recovery goes well."

"Thanks."

As she started to go out the door she turned around and said, "I do love you, Turner."

"Maybe. But to really love someone, you have to trust. And you made it clear you don't."

Anger flashed in her eyes. "You don't get to tell me what's real and what isn't. I know what I feel for you and it's as real as it gets." He started to speak but she was on a roll. "You have no clue how it feels to be left because you're inadequate. Because you can't give a man what he wants. You have no idea how it feels to *be* inadequate."

"You're not. You're buying into what your bastard ex said to you. He's the one who was lacking, not you."

"That's not what it feels like," she said, and walked out the door. Out of his life.

And he only had himself to blame.

Chapter Eighteen

TURNER THOUGHT ABOUT skipping poker night at the McBride ranch that month, but he really had nothing better to do. And he knew his family would give him shit if he bailed. He just hoped they wouldn't harass him about Charlie. But that was probably a futile hope.

Besides, his parents weren't there and their long-time housekeeper, Ruby, had promised to make her famous pot roast, vegetables and homemade rolls. Turner really liked pot roast, but he could eat his weight in rolls. Over dinner they talked about Jessie's plan to expand her horse business. Realizing they weren't going to bring up Charlie, he relaxed.

He couldn't keep his mind on the game. He thought about the apple pie Ruby had served. It was good, one of her specialties. But it made him think about Charlie. Crap, everything made him think about Charlie.

He was fairly certain he'd lost weight since Charlie wasn't bringing him food anymore. He hadn't been to the pie shop either, although he'd come close to breaking several times. And not solely because of the pie.

Maybe he was being too much of a hard-ass. Maybe he should have just taken her at her word. Maybe—

"Turner, what the hell is going on with you?" Spencer asked. "If you're going to play, pay attention."

"Sorry. Fold." He couldn't even blame his inattention on pain medicine since all he was taking now was over the counter. His ribs still hurt like a bitch, but his arm was less painful as long as he kept it in the sling.

They finished that hand, which Jessie, naturally, won. "Before we start again," Jessie said, looking at Turner, "what are you going to do about Charlie?"

And there it was. "I don't want to talk about it."

Graham, Spencer and Jessie all regarded him with varying degrees of disapproval. Graham said, "I don't get it. She told me at the hospital that she loved you. Didn't she tell you she loved you?"

He shoved a hand through his hair. "Yes. But not until after the accident."

"So? She says she loves you. And I know you're still in love with her or you wouldn't be such a pain in the ass. So what's the problem?"

"How dense are you?" Turner asked. "Charlie was simply reacting to the accident. She doesn't really love me. Hell, she freaked the minute I told her I loved her. And that wasn't even three weeks before I got hit by that truck."

"Oh, man," Spencer said, shaking his head. "I'd say you're the dense one."

"Agree," Graham said.

"Yup," Jessie said. "Completely clueless."

"I don't remember asking for input from any of you," he snarled.

"Tough shit," Spencer said. "You're getting it."

"I'm sure she gave you a reason when she broke up with you," Jessie said.

"She didn't exactly break up with me."

"What the hell does that mean?" Spencer asked.

"I told you she freaked out after I told her I loved her. She decided that we needed to take a break so I could think about—" He broke off since he couldn't talk about the real reason she'd wanted him to think.

"Think about what?" Jessie asked.

"I can't talk about it. It's private. But it doesn't matter. She doesn't trust me so how can she really love me?"

"Go talk to her, Turner," Jessie said. "You're both miserable. Fix it."

"Charlie's miserable? How do you know?"

"I talked to her at the shop today. Trust me, she's as miserable as you are. Go fix this."

"It's not that easy. I don't know how to make it right."

"You're a smart guy," Jessie told him. "Usually. You'll figure it out. And in the meantime, pay up."

"I can't muck out stalls," he said, glad for once of his injuries.

"That's okay. I'll think of something," his sister told him.

"Yeah, that's what I'm afraid of."

CHARLIE WALKED INTO the Millennial Village Apartments and stopped at the intercom. She squared her shoulders. She would have preferred to surprise Turner, but that wasn't possible now. If she still had her key, she wouldn't have to go through this step. Somehow, she was going to make Turner believe that she really did love him. That she really did trust him. She wasn't sure how, not yet, but she wasn't giving up without trying again. And again, if necessary. It had been three weeks since his accident. More than two since he'd kicked her out of his apartment and told her not to come back. He'd had time to think about things. And to feel better. Maybe he'd listen to her this time.

She punched the intercom and waited. "It's Charlie," she said when he answered. "I need to see you."

"I'll be right down."

A few minutes later the elevator doors slid open. He wore an old Houston Astros T-shirt and old, faded jeans with a hole in the knee that she knew came from wear and tear and not as a fashion statement. His arm was casted and in a sling but he looked like he felt 100 percent better than he had the last time she'd seen him.

Best of all he looked happy to see her.

"Hey," he said.

"Hey."

"I'm glad you came."

"You are?"

"Yes." He took her hand and pulled her close. "If you hadn't come to me, I'd have come to you."

She stared into his eyes. "Why?" she whispered.

He let go of her hand and cupped her face. And then he smiled and kissed her. Surprise held her still. Then she simply melted. It was only a kiss, a simple laying of his lips on hers, but it felt so good, so right and she realized how desperately she'd missed him.

In the elevator, he kissed her again. And again in the hallway leading to his apartment. Once inside, he put his good arm around her and kissed her. Hot, hard, and with purpose. "Wait," she gasped when he let her up for air. "I need to talk to you."

"Am I going to like it?"

"I hope so."

"Can it wait?"

"No. I need to say what I came over here to say."

He sighed. "All right." He led her to the couch and they both sat.

"I came to tell you one more time that I love you. And I do trust you. But I understand why you think I don't. Will you let me explain?"

"You don't need to explain—"

"Yes I do." She held up a hand so he wouldn't interrupt her. "I can't say that your accident made no difference because it did. It made me realize there are no guarantees in life. I never thought I'd have a hysterectomy before I was thirty, but I did. I didn't expect my husband to walk out on me once he knew I couldn't have his children. But that's what happened."

"You're well rid of the bastard."

"I know. But it left a mark. It took me a long time to get over the divorce. To come to terms with the certainty that I'd never have a baby. I thought I had. But I hadn't. That's why I wouldn't date anyone I thought might get serious. And it was why I was afraid to date you. I knew with you, it would be different. I couldn't give you the chance to hurt me. I couldn't make myself that vulnerable. Even though I know you, and know what kind of person you are, I wasn't the same woman. All I could see was what I couldn't give you. What I couldn't give me."

"Charlie, I just want *you*. I don't care if we ever have kids. If we adopt, that's great. I'll love them and enjoy them. But if we never have any, I'll still be happy because I'll have you. You're the person who matters to me."

"We're talking like we're getting married. We haven't even gotten back together yet. I wouldn't have told you about my hysterectomy so soon but I didn't think it was fair to let you—to let us—grow any closer without letting you know something so important."

"It wasn't that soon. And I had just told you I loved you. You were right to tell me the truth." He leaned forward and kissed her. "I was about to go to you and tell you I was a fool and beg you to let me back in your life. Whatever happens, I want to be with you, Charlie."

"Oh, Turner. I want to be with you, too." She put her arms around his neck and kissed him.

He returned the kiss, their tongues touching and retreating, the kisses growing more heated by the moment.

Charlie pulled back and asked, "How are your ribs?"

"Not good enough to carry you into the bedroom, but plenty good enough to make love."

He took off his sling and she helped him off with his T-shirt, carefully, since he had to work his broken arm out of the sleeve. He tried to help her take off her sweater but he wasn't much use one-handed. She laughed and stripped it off and followed with her bra. She went to work on his jeans, unbuttoning, unzipping, sliding her hand inside his boxers to feel him hot, hard and ready for her.

"You're killing me."

She froze. "What did I do? Did I hurt your ribs?"

He laughed. "My ribs are fine. But there's another part of me that needs serious attention."

She looked down and smiled. "So I see." She stood, undid her jeans, pushed them down her legs and stepped out of them. Next, she got rid of her panties, watching Turner work his way out of his jeans and boxers, which he managed surprisingly fast one-handed. He held out his hand and she took it, and straddled his lap. She put her arms around his neck. "I missed you." She kissed him and said against his lips, "So much."

"I missed you too."

They were too impatient to wait long. She lifted herself up and sank back down, gasping as he filled her. Their gazes locked as she slowly began to ride. His hand on her hip guided her as the sweet rhythm intensified. He slipped his hand between their bodies, stroking her, pushing her higher, higher still until she came apart with a cry. Moments later, he followed. She collapsed against him before she remembered.

Quickly, she pulled her upper body back. "I didn't mean to do that."

"You're fine." He held her close and whispered in her ear, "Better than fine."

She drew back enough to see his face and laid her palm against his cheek. "I love you, Turner."

He turned his head to kiss her palm. "I love you, too. Will you marry me?"

She stared at him. "Are you serious?"

"I've never been more serious or certain in my life. Marry me, Charlie. Let me love you and have you love me for the rest of our lives."

"I love you."

"That's not an answer."

"Yes, Turner, I'll marry you."

"No doubts?"

"Not one," she said, and kissed him.

The End

If you enjoyed this book, please leave a review at your favorite online retailer! Even if it's just a sentence or two it makes all the difference.

Thanks for reading *Texas on My Mind* by Eve Gaddy!

Discover your next romance at TulePublishing.com.

TULE
PUBLISHING

If you enjoyed *Texas on My Mind,*
you'll love the next book in….

The Heart of Texas series

Book 1: *Heart of the Texas Doctor*

Book 2: *Texas on My Mind*

Book 3: *Under the Mistletoe*

Book 4: *Coming soon!*

Available now at your favorite online retailer!

More books by Eve Gaddy

The Gallaghers of Montana series

Book 1: *Sing Me Back Home*

Book 2: *Love Me, Cowgirl*

Book 3: *The Doctor's Christmas Proposal*

Book 4: *The Cowboy and the Doctor*

Book 5: *Return of the Cowgirl*

The Devil's Rock at Whiskey River series

Book 1: *Rebel Pilot Texas Doctor*

Book 2: *His Best Friend's Sister*

Book 3: *No Ordinary Texas Billionaire*

Available now at your favorite online retailer!

About the Author

Eve Gaddy is the best-selling award-winning author of more than seventeen novels. Her books have won and been nominated for awards from Romantic Times, Golden Quill, Bookseller's Best, Holt Medallion, Texas Gold, Daphne Du Maurier and more. She was nominated for a Romantic Times Career Achievement Award for Innovative Series romance as well as winning the 2008 Romantic Times Career Achievement award for Series Storyteller of the year. Eve's books have sold over a million copies worldwide and been published in many foreign countries. Eve lives in East Texas with her husband of many years.

Thank you for reading

Texas on My Mind

If you enjoyed this book, you can find more from all our great authors at TulePublishing.com, or from your favorite online retailer.

TULE
PUBLISHING

Made in the USA
Columbia, SC
31 October 2021